THE SECRET AGENT

Two days after September 11, 2001, an intelligence officer from the South African Secret Service arrived in Washington, D.C. Three months later he was responsible for the arrest of Richard Reid, the notorious British *al-Qaeda* operative . . . A series of short stories follow secret agent Jackson from Boston to Oxford, Quebec City, the Italian Alps, and his final and most deadly mission four months after his premature retirement.

Books by Rafe McGregor in the Linford Mystery Library:

THE SECRET SERVICE
THE SECRET POLICEMAN

RAFE McGREGOR

THE SECRET AGENT

Complete and Unabridged

LINFORD
Leicester

First published in Great Britain in 2007

First Linford Edition
published 2008

British Library CIP Data

McGregor, Rafe
The secret agent.—Large print ed.—
Linford mystery library
1. Detective and mystery stories, English
2. Large type books
I. Title
823.9′2 [F]

ISBN 978–1–84782–371–7

Published by
F. A. Thorpe (Publishing)
Anstey, Leicestershire

Set by Words & Graphics Ltd.
Anstey, Leicestershire
Printed and bound in Great Britain by
T. J. International Ltd., Padstow, Cornwall

This book is printed on acid-free paper

To:
Steven Cross, the Blue Knight.

Two

Constable Ludlow watched his new partner return to the cruiser. She was kinda easy on the eye, if you didn't mind the nose and the severe haircut. Not that it mattered. She was tall and strong, and she carried herself well in the body armour. That mattered. She still looked like a nineteen year old girl. That mattered too. At nineteen and nine months she was probably the youngest officer out on patrol in the whole damn Regiment. Some civilians wouldn't respond well to that. She climbed back in the cruiser, removed her cap, and buckled her seatbelt. 'Ready?' Ludlow asked. She nodded. 'Good. Book us back from our Ten-Sixty-Two, and get the map out.'

Ashley Brown keyed the mainset radio mike and informed Dispatch that Eight-Bravo-Twelve — Battlefords Rural Detachment car twelve — was now back from their meal break. Ludlow pulled out into the traffic, and headed north. Ashley removed the road atlas from the storage compartment in the passenger door. Ludlow had told her that the cruiser was their office. Everything in it had a place where it belonged, so you knew where it was if you needed it in a hurry. She started flicking through the pages to find their current location.

'We're taking a drive out to Delmas. I want ya to follow the route out to the highway on the map, and make sure ya know where we're at. OK?'

'Yes, OK.'

'Your work on the radio is good, but you're gonna keep at it. It's your baby now and I won't be touching it unless you're out the car. By the time we've finished your mentorship, you're gonna be an A-number-one crew. What did I tell ya about crewing yesterday?'

'A good crew does everything but drive,' Ashley replied. She liked it when he said 'we'. It made her feel less like a schoolkid and more like a law enforcement officer.

'Yup. And as you saw when we

responded to that Ten-Eighteen, it ain't as easy as it looks. We're moving fast and you gotta listen to the radio, talk on the radio, operate the siren, and sometimes give directions. Also, you gotta keep your eyes open. It can get hectic. I'm so used to driving now that it don't get in the way of my observation. That'll come with time. But it's not just these,' he pointed to his eyes, 'it's your ears and your nose ya gotta use as well.'

Ashley had already noticed that Ludlow rarely looked at her when he spoke. He was continually scanning the vehicles and pedestrians they passed. She turned back to the map. She knew which onramp Ludlow would use, but hadn't worked out which route he was taking.

'That brings me to our patrolling. Ya see lotsa cops driving with their windows up. You'll see I only do it when it's raining or snowing. Why do ya think?'

Ashley pondered for a few seconds, then answered, 'Because you can't hear anything if the window's up?'

'Yup. Can't smell nothing neither, and your peripheral vision ain't as good.

Peripheral vision is important. There's another reason too. Less likely to happen, but real important if it does. Any ideas?'

Ashley shook her head, 'No.'

'If the cruiser takes a hit with a rifle, the bullet'll go through the thin metal of the door like it ain't even there. Put a piece of glass in the middle, and you got a good chance it'll either deflect elsewhere, or slow down so's it don't do much damage by the time it gets to us.'

Ashley found it hard to believe, but she had no reason to doubt Tom, and she didn't see him as the type to joke about important stuff like that. Either way, she hoped she never had to find out.

'You found us yet?' he asked.

'Yes. Next left and we merge onto the highway — I think.' She waited nervously for his reply.

'Yup. How ya carrying?'

'One-up, hammer down, safety off. Just like you told me.'

'Good. Never mind the Depot nonsense. Your piece must always be ready to fire. If ya don't want an accidental discharge . . . ' he paused for her to finish.

'Don't pull the trigger,' Ashley knew she had that one right.

'Yup. I taught ya another thing about firearms yesterday, when someone's aiming one at ya. Ya remember that as well?'

'Yes. Always make yourself as small a target as possible. That means keeping low, standing side-on, or getting into the blind spot on a vehicle stop. Target displacement.'

'Yup. Good, good. Ya can add the four reasons to keep your window down to yesterday's lesson, and I figure that's enough for now. Let's get the rest of day two out the way first. We got our nights tomorrow. We'll probably get some time to work through things in the early hours. Keep us awake if it's quiet.' Ludlow indicated and eased the Crown onto Highway 16. 'While we're cruising I want you to get used to looking at the cars with your eyes and listening to the radio with your ears. When ya get good at it ya won't miss the APBs anymore, like ya just did.'

'Sorry — what — '

'Never mind. Don't apologise and don't be shy. Get onto Dispatch and ask them to repeat. Just make sure ya write it down, otherwise you'll forget.'

Ashley did as she was told and repeated the details to Ludlow: 'Blue Honda Accord, registration Bravo-Foxtrot-Kilo-One-Nine-Five; two white male suspects wanted for a robbery at ISM Canada in Regina an hour and a half ago; walked in with an assault rifle and a shopping trolley, stole CD-roms and hard drives; last seen heading in the direction of Highway 11; Ten-Thirty-Six, Ten-Sixty. Also a white pickup truck — registration unknown — seen in the vicinity, two white male occupants behaving suspiciously.'

'Ya remember those codes?'

'Yes, 'armed suspects' and 'use extreme caution'.'

'Yup. Good. That took a while to get to us, and it's miles away, so it musta been something big. Why would ya rob a computer company at gunpoint?'

Ashley wasn't sure if Ludlow was testing her again, or just asking a question. 'Everyone worries about hackers breaking into online programs, but all the information in those programs has to be stored somewhere on hard copy. If you know where they're stored, you don't need to be able to hack, you can just walk in and pick them up.' Ludlow glanced at her. 'What?' she asked.

'I like that. What have ya just told me?'

'I, I'm not — '

'You've just told me there's an inside man — or woman. You're thinking like a cop. Good, good. Remember something else I said yesterday: don't be afraid to speak up if ya see something that ain't right. See, hear, or smell. I'm in charge, but you're a constable just the same as me and I ain't so good I can see everything. If ya find us something, we'll follow it up. If ya don't, it'll be part of your learning curve. But don't be shy.'

Ashley smiled, 'I won't.' She liked Tom. He was a short, bulky man with a shaved head and a bushy moustache. He reminded her of her dad. He was also a cop and —

'Did you say a blue Accord?' Ludlow interrupted her thoughts.

'I . . . er — yes.'

Ludlow indicated and overtook the car in front. 'Two cars up ahead. Looked like two occupants, and the plate started with bravo. Let's take a look.'

Ashley felt a rush of excitement, like she had yesterday when Tom told her to put the blue lights and siren on. 'Bravo-Foxtrot-Kilo-One-Nine-Five.' She looked at Ludlow: he was focused on the Accord up ahead. It was moving fast, but they were gaining.

'No need to rush,' Ludlow said. 'We'll reel them in slow. What can ya see?'

'Er . . . bravo, foxtrot, kilo, one, nine — it's them! It's the car from Regina! I — '

'Take it easy. I'm gonna hang back until you've let Dispatch know where we are, and if we got any back-up. Go on, nice and slow. We got all the time in the world.'

Ashley could feel her heart beating faster as it pumped more blood out to her muscles, lungs, and brain. She fought to keep calm as she relayed the message. The reply was Ten-Twelve, one: standby, one minute.

Ludlow saw Ashley's right hand move towards her holster. 'If ya feel more comfortable with your piece out, now's as good a time as any. Just keep it pointed at the floor, and keep your finger off the trigger.' She did. 'It don't sound like we got anyone nearby. If that's the case, we're gonna have to pull him. There's two of them and two of us, so we'll be OK. Ya know what to do?'

'Yes.'

'Eight-Bravo-Twelve, Four-One-Six.'

Ashley responded, 'Go!'

'That's a negative. Ten-Twenty-Six, twenty mikes.'

'Tell them we'll take it,' said Ludlow.

'Ten-Four, Four-One-Six. We are going to Ten-Eleven, over.'

'Received. Code Five. Repeat: Code Five.'

'Ten-Four, Four-One-Six.' Code Five: stop at gunpoint. Ashley noticed that Ludlow had eased his own Smith & Wesson from his holster, and tucked it under his right thigh.

'When I tell ya, hit the lights and give them a quick burst with the wail so they know we're here. Remember, we're on the highway and it's noisy. When we stop, I'll use the PA to give the commands. But as soon as we stop I want ya out and covering the passenger side. You'll have space, so use that blind spot. Don't shoot unless ya see a firearm, but if ya see a firearm, don't hesitate. Whatever happens, make sure ya shout me. OK?'

Ashley's heart was pounding like a hammer and she was sweating despite the open window. Her mouth was dry. She tasted her lunch starting to come up, and swallowed hard. 'Yes, Tom, I'm OK.'

'Then cock your piece, and let's pull them.' Ludlow moved up behind the Accord. Ashley flicked the siren switch on and then off. The Accord slowed, indicated right, and moved over into the rescue lane. 'Tell Dispatch where we've stopped,' Ludlow told her. For the first time since he'd seen the car, he felt a bead of sweat on his forehead. Something was wrong. Ashley finished her transmission. The Accord came to a halt. Ludlow braked, and stopped fifteen yards behind it.

He whipped up the handbrake, ‘Now!’

Ludlow gripped his nine-millimetre with his right hand as he opened the door with his left. He grabbed the PA mike as he slid from the car, crouching behind the door for cover. Ashley was nowhere to be seen. She’d moved fast. Good. ‘Stay where ya are, do not move unless instructed,’ he said over the PA. ‘Both of ya put your hands up on the dash, where I can see ’em. Passenger, keep your hands where they are. Driver, switch off the engine.’

Ludlow looked over the front sight of his pistol. He saw the car shudder once, and then go still. ‘Now, very slowly, put the keys on the roof. Bring both palms up so I can see ’em. Open your door from the outside.’

The driver complied — exactly. Something *was* wrong.

Ashley was kneeling half a dozen yards from the cruiser, with the passenger’s head in her pistol sights. He’d placed his hands on the dashboard as instructed, but otherwise he was motionless. Her heart was still thumping, but she was back in control. Her hands were dead steady. And Tom was right: when she'd told the passenger he was covered, she knew he couldn't see her. She was low in his blind spot. She'd done exactly as she'd been told and the Code Five was going exactly as planned. She used her peripheral vision to scan the driver and the back of the car. No movement there either.

'Put your palms on your head and stand up slowly.' Ludlow dropped the mike and aimed his pistol with both hands. The driver complied again. He was tall and skinny with a scruffy goatee, wore jeans and a baggy shirt. Ludlow shouted to make himself heard above the traffic, 'Walk to the rear of the car. Turn around and place your palms flat on the trunk.' Ludlow knew these were the perps. No doubt. So why the hell were they coming so quietly? He stood, kept his pistol on the suspect, and moved around the door.

Ashley kept her sights trained on the passenger. She saw the driver get out and walk to the back of the car. He put his hands flat on the trunk. It would be her turn to give the commands shortly. Just like at the Academy. She knew what she was doing and she was confident now. Ludlow moved into her peripheral vision, covering the driver. She heard a car door open.

She had not seen a car door open.

Adrenalin flooded her veins. Time slowed. Should she shout Tom? No, not yet. She wasn't sure yet. Ashley's vision was narrowing, but she managed to keep her suspect in sight as she turned her head to the left.

A white pickup had stopped behind the cruiser. Two men were debussing. Detectives? Too scruffy. Plainclothes? Maybe — '

The driver of the pickup raised a rifle.

'Tom!' Ashley spun on her knee, bringing the pistol around and squeezing the trigger.

Ludlow turned to Ashley — caught sight of the pickup — saw the Accord driver dive to the ground. He was in-between two perps. He knew he wasn't quick enough to survive this. He fired twice at the suspect in front, gritting his teeth against the bullet he knew was coming from behind.

Ashley was deafened as three handguns went off simultaneously.

She fired again, then a third and fourth shot. The rifleman bellowed, staggered back, and collapsed next to the truck. She saw Ludlow go down to her right, and the pickup passenger turn his gun on her. She heard another door open behind her. She knew it was the passenger from the Accord.

Time seemed to stop.

Ashley sat back on her rump and fired at the pickup passenger. She heard a gunshot behind her, twisted, and rolled onto her stomach. She looked up at the barrel of a pistol sticking out from the Accord. She fired three rounds at the body behind it. Then she flipped over onto her back and aimed at the pickup. Again.

No one was there.

Ashley tilted her head to look at the Accord. No one there either. She clenched her stomach muscles and sat up. Both men from the pickup were down. Both men from the Accord were down. So was Ludlow. She ran to him.

He was on his back, bleeding badly. 'Leave me. Get the perps' weapons clear!'

Ashley moved to the closest suspect, and pulled his pistol from his belt. As she moved to the next, she keyed her handset mike: 'Four-One-Six, Eight-Bravo-Twelve. Officer down, officer down!'

Clock Work

'You will use the name John Daniel,' said the tall, clean-cut blonde from behind her desk. 'Put your bag down. Sit.'

Her visitor nodded once, and did both.

'What have you been told?' she asked.

'Yesterday I was called to the director general's office. His secretary instructed me to take the twenty-fifteen South African Airways flight to Heathrow and report to you, here, as soon as possible.'

'That's it?'

'*Ja*.'

'Good. You'll be needing these,' she stood, took a black leather wallet out of a drawer, and picked up a briefcase Daniel hadn't noticed. She brought both around to him. 'You're a South African born British subject working as a security manager for Exall, Guest, and Cotterall, an auditing firm in Canary Wharf. You live in Putney. The cover won't hold, but you won't need it to.'

Daniel checked the wallet. There was a debit card, two credit cards, a full UK driver's licence with his photo on it, and a hundred pounds in cash. There were also two train tickets with today's date on them, one for the Underground, and one to Oxford. He stood up and pocketed the wallet.

She continued, 'Be very careful with the briefcase. Make sure you're alone when you open it. All the information is there. The combination has been set to your code. You're booked into Linton Lodge in Oxford. It's a Best Western about a mile from the city centre. You have a meeting with an access agent at seven o'clock tonight. Any questions?'

'Not if it's all in there,' Daniel indicated the briefcase.

'It is. Everything you'll need for the job. And remember, this is from the director general himself.'

'Then I'll get started,' Daniel slung his sports bag over his shoulder, and picked up the briefcase. He was surprised when she wished him good luck. Daniel had grown out of the habit of smiling since the scar, so he just nodded again and left.

The door opened with a plastic key, which was unfortunate from a security point of view. Daniel put the briefcase and the bag on the bed. He checked the wardrobe wasn't fixed, then shifted it until a few inches blocked the door. He returned to the briefcase, laid it on the desk, and caught his reflection in the mirror. He looked as tired as he felt. He glanced at his watch: quarter past twelve. No wonder, he'd been in Johannesburg sixteen hours ago, and Pretoria three before that.

He manipulated the combinations on the briefcase, clicked the switches, and opened it. Inside the top half he found a pistol and a hand grenade. They were held in place in the foam rubber lining with plastic ties. Below: a handgun cleaning kit; a mission briefing consisting of five loose sheets of A4 paper; ten A5-size colour photographs; an Oxford A-Z; a bus ticket and timetable for the Airline Company bus from Oxford to Gatwick; and an airplane ticket for a Lufthansa flight from Gatwick to Berlin, leaving at midnight tomorrow.

A murder kit complete with instructions.

The mission brief was divided into five sections: Agent Cover, Target Information, Target Confirmation, Target Execution, and Agent Extraction.

The target was a thirty-four year old South African citizen named Siyabonga Mchunu. Daniel recognised the name immediately. Colonel Mchunu had been adjutant to Lieutenant General Mthimkulu, the Chief of the South African Army. Last year he'd been investigated for fraud before deciding to leave the country in a hurry with a large amount of Department of Defence money that didn't belong to him. Daniel remembered communiqués placing him first in Abu Dhabi and then Switzerland. The ID photo clipped to the second page was unnecessary, as were the A5 photographs; he hadn't altered his appearance.

Daniel had two questions: why were the Secret Service using an intelligence officer instead of an agent, and why did they want Mchunu dead? If the Secret Service had to hunt down everyone who defrauded the government, they'd need a full time death squad and plenty of dissembling diplomats for the subsequent denials. His second question was answered in the last paragraph of the second page.

The president's granddaughter had recently suffered a nervous breakdown. This was common knowledge. During psychotherapy she'd told her therapist that Mchunu had raped her five years ago. She'd kept quiet about it because her grandfather had been up for re-election at the time and she'd wanted to avoid any scandal. She still didn't want anyone to know, but the therapist had taken the news straight to the president. Absconding with hundreds of thousand of Rand was one thing, but raping the president's granddaughter was guaranteed to reduce one's life expectancy. Drastically. Daniel thought it was probably the reason Mchunu had taken the money and run. Not that he cared. He was just there to do a job.

But he still wondered why he'd been selected for it. Despite the misconception propagated by the mass media, intelligence officers didn't go about breaking and entering, stealing secret documents, or killing people. They recruited intelligence agents to do that for them, and thus remained once-removed from the actual dirty work. Perhaps there was a shortage of suitable agents for the job, although Daniel found that unlikely with something like three million expatriate South Africans in Britain. Maybe there wasn't one who could be trusted to keep his mouth shut if he was caught. That was more like it.

The access agent's name was Lily. Daniel didn't remember her from his tour with the Economic Reconnaissance Office in South Africa House. She must be new. Her profession was listed as prostitute, which was unusual. Access agents were routinely of high social standing, people who assisted intelligence officers to recruit suitable and useful agents. Daniel was to meet her in The Turf at seven tonight. She would find him. He looked at the mirror again, saw the thick, white scar that ran from his left eye, down the side of his cheek, almost to his mouth.

Ja, she probably would.

Daniel woke at five. He dressed quickly, left the hotel, and walked into Jericho, a small suburb of Victorian terraced houses immediately to the north-west of the city centre. The target execution was scheduled for the corner of Cranham Terrace and Jericho Street, outside a pub called the Harcourt Arms. The pub was right on the corner, at the end of a terrace row. Opposite the entrance, across the narrow street, a beech tree grew out of the pavement. Daniel committed the terrain to memory, but was careful to keep moving so as not to draw attention to himself.

Thirty minutes later, he found The Turf, hidden away in an ancient alley off New College Lane. The pub was a long, low building with a raised section serving food at the far end. It was busy, but not full. Most of the clientele looked like students. Wealthy students. Daniel ordered a pint of Hoegaarden blonde beer and took a stool along the wall. He wasn't a great reader, but regretted not bringing a book to the pub. It seemed quite a normal thing to do in England, particularly here in a university town, and he had no idea how long Lily was going to be.

'*Howzit*, do you mind if I join you?' the woman stood very close to him, almost touching.

'No, please do.' She was short and slim, with skin the colour of milky coffee, long curly black hair, and bright red lips. She could have been anything from fifteen to thirty. She smoothed her short skirt over her thighs as she sat. 'Would you like a drink?' Daniel asked.

'No, thanks, I doubt you're gonna make it worth my while.' Her accent was South African. Daniel guessed Cape Town. 'My name's Lily, by the way,' she held out her hand.

Daniel took it. 'John. I'm afraid you're right about me not making it worth your while. Is this your regular place?'

'*Ja*, I pick up tourists or students here.'

'The manager doesn't mind?'

She smiled at him, 'My customers don't complain, John. I'm good for business, not bad. In a few minutes I'm going to move on and mingle, cos that's what I usually do.'

'Okay, do you have a message for me?'

'*Ja*, the message is that you have confirmation.'

'That's all?'

'That's it.'

'Is he expecting to meet you?'

'No, he's expecting a man.'

'Good.'

'Lovey, that's very sweet of you, but neither of us has time to chat, do we?' She smiled at him again, squeezed his forearm gently as she rose, and moved off to a table with three young men.

Daniel finished his pint without hurrying. When he left, Lily was still at the table with the three men, a glass of white wine in front of her.

The pistol was an HS95, a Croatian imitation of the famous Swiss SIG Sauer nine millimetre. Daniel removed it from the briefcase, leaving a handgun-shaped space in the foam rubber. It reminded him of the old toy he'd had as a child where you had to put the right block into the right hole. Except that this was a little more obvious. He slid the magazine from the pistol's grip. He removed the bullets, placing each on the desk top, and counted sixteen. He checked the chamber: empty. He opened the cleaning kit, and began disassembling the pistol. He wasn't happy about having to use a weapon he hadn't actually fired, but he had no choice.

There was no choice in any of it. Every detail of the murder had been pre-planned and prearranged, even down to the specifics. The briefcase contained everything he needed: information, instructions, and tools for both the assassination and the escape. It was like those colouring-in books from junior primary. What were they called . . . colour by numbers? *Ja*, colour by number. All Daniel had to do was turn up in the right place at the right time, and follow instructions. He was purely a tool, no more and no less than the pistol provided.

Murder by numbers.

He finished field-stripping the pistol, cleaned the separate parts, and checked the firing pin. Then he re-assembled it, using an oiled cloth to prevent leaving fingerprints. He replaced the empty magazine, and dry fired double-action: click. Perfect. Next, he loaded the magazine, slid it back into place, cocked a round into the chamber, and eased the hammer down. He flicked the safety catch on, wiped the outside of the pistol with a clean cloth, and put it back in the briefcase.

The hand grenade was an HG85, British Army standard issue. It was an incendiary model, which meant that the forty-nine millimetre aluminium case was filled with thermite instead of steel balls. The thermite would burn for forty seconds at around four thousand degrees Fahrenheit. It would ignite everything it came into contact with, including metal. The detonator was fitted with the standard four second fuse. Daniel removed the extra safety clip and returned the grenade to the briefcase.

The plane ticket was in his own name. John Daniel would cease to exist once he left the Linton Lodge tomorrow morning. He checked the bus timetable and ran through the plan in his head. Mchunu was meeting him opposite the Harcourt

Arms at eight tomorrow night. He would pull up next to the tree in his black Citroen C5. He would be alone. Daniel would shoot him as he exited the car, push him back in, and administer the *coup de grâce*. Then he would throw in both pistol and grenade, and flee on foot to Gloucester Green bus station. Busses left at eight-thirty and nine o'clock. The flight left at midnight. It was as simple as that. The straightforward plans tended to work the best: there was less that could go wrong.

Like clockwork.

Daniel opened his window and burned each A4 page and each A5 photo, transferring the remains from the ashtray to the toilet when he was finished. He'd already found a skip to dump the briefcase and sports bag when he checked out. He switched on the TV as he undressed, thinking about morality. It hadn't even occurred to him not to kill Mchunu. Had he left his morals behind when he'd joined the Secret Service, or had it been before that, in his previous life? He couldn't remember.

At a quarter to eight Daniel was in the small, Victorian cemetery of St Sepulchre's, at the other end of Cranham Terrace. There were no benches, so he sat on the raised stone of John Wilson, a porter who'd died a hundred and fifty four years ago. He'd been aged seventy. Daniel wondered if he would live that long himself.

He was wearing a reversible weatherproof parka, with the black inner lining on the outside. In the poacher's pocket — unzipped — was the hand grenade. Daniel's passport and plane ticket were in the inaccessible pockets on the other side. His hands were snug inside a pair of tight-fitting dark blue police marksman's gloves. He wore stretch denims and brown hiking boots. The denims held his wallet and bus ticket. The pistol, safety catch off, was tucked into his belt, just to the right of the buckle, concealed by the jacket.

He glanced at his watch, stood up slowly, and walked out into Walton Street.

Two minutes past eight: Daniel was standing in the doorway of 4 Cranham

Terrace, facing the bright blue door. He was nestled in shadow, out of the light from the Harcourt Arms. The beech tree — across the road — was fifteen metres away. The street was quiet, except for the occasional car or pedestrian. Two women strode past him without a glance. They went into the pub, two doors down. Daniel waited.

A car slowed, and stopped next to the tree: a black Citroen.

Daniel took the pistol from his trousers, and cocked the hammer back. The car door opened. Daniel took a deep breath and walked into the road. He kept the pistol low, gripping it lightly with both hands. A tall black man climbed out the car. Daniel stopped five metres away. He slid into a side-on stance and raised the pistol. He looked over the front sight and squeezed the trigger once.

Click.

Mchunu was facing Daniel. Both men reached inside their jackets as Daniel dived behind the Citroen. His pistol clattered uselessly on the road. He landed heavily, using his left arm to break his fall as his right removed the grenade from his pocket. He crouched against the corner of the car and twisted the pin out. Mchunu's first shot cracked over the boot.

One second.

Daniel scrabbled round to the passenger side of the car, keeping low. The second shot lodged in the boot.

Two seconds.

Daniel heard Mchunu move and saw the muzzle-flash of the third shot. His heart thundered a relentless tattoo. He crouched even lower and backed around the bonnet, keeping his head down.

Three seconds.

Mchunu stepped from the rear of the car onto the pavement. He saw Daniel. Daniel lobbed the grenade high. Mchunu fired. Daniel threw himself under the engine block.

Four seconds.

The grenade detonated into the night, and the thermite illuminated the entire street. Daniel waited a single second, then leapt to his feet. The tree and the Citroen were both burning. So were two cars parked outside the pub, and a garage door at the end of the terrace. As Daniel jumped back he smelled the burning flesh. He heard the sizzling and crackling of Mchunu's torso as his body flamed. There was nothing where his head had been.

Daniel turned and sprinted down Hart Street.

Right, into Cardigan Street, then left into Albert. He bumped into a couple on the corner, kept moving.

He crossed Clarendon Street, crossed Wellington, sprinted past the new synagogue and the Lebanese restaurant.

Richmond Road, then hard right into Worcester Place.

Daniel slowed, and stopped outside a wooden door set into the high wall on his right. He checked up and down the street, saw no one, and opened the door. He stepped inside a small, overgrown garden behind another row of terraces. He took off his gloves, threw them away, and reversed his parka. He stood in the cold for a full minute before putting the beige jacket back on. He fought to breathe through his nose and stomach, gradually slowing his heart rate. Composed, he walked casually out into Worcester Place, careful not to touch the door with his fingers.

Twenty-three minutes past eight: Daniel was standing in Bay 7, under the long bus shelter at Gloucester Green. There were ten buses in the dozen bays, but the eight-thirty to Gatwick hadn't arrived yet. Daniel noticed movement to his left and turned to see two policemen walking through the crowd. One had a Heckler & Koch submachine gun, the other appeared unarmed. They were in Bay 3. He looked to his right, and saw another two in Bay 11. Also one armed, one not.

Daniel stayed where he was.

The policemen on the left were moving quicker. They were looking at everyone in the crowd. He checked the right again: they had reached Bay 10. They both stopped, and the unarmed one spoke to a man in a leather jacket.

Twenty-four minutes past eight: the Airline Company bus pulled up. Daniel was fourth in the queue. As the doors opened, the two policemen came up from the left. They stood at the entrance to the bus. Everyone in the queue was staring at them. Daniel was careful to do the same.

No one moved.

The first passenger climbed on, then the second. As the third followed, the unarmed policeman put his hand out in front of Daniel.

'Hold it.'

The armed policeman walked in front of him to Bay 8.

'Thank you,' said his colleague as he followed.

Daniel stepped onto the bus.

Contre Temps

'Whoa, it aint ten-eighteen.'

Megan Brown knew she was driving the unmarked Chevy Caprice too fast as she sped towards the airport. She forced herself to slow down and control her emotions. 'Sorry.'

'Eh?' asked Staff Sergeant Gaffney.

Megan didn't want to tell him, but she knew he wouldn't leave it alone. 'It's just this place.'

'Quebec City?'

'The whole damn province. These fucking Quebeckers really piss me off. We're supposed to be a bilingual country. Do you see any signs in English, cos I don't? They all speak it better than we do French, but they won't use it. And I bet they'll be out burning the flag again, tonight, just like they did last Canada Day. I mean, who the hell do they think they are?'

'Don't let it bother you.' Gaffney was a

man of few words.

'I can't help it. Today is the day for all Canadians to be proud of their country. I swear I'm gonna shoot someone tonight. Why don't we let them secede if that's what they want? See how long they last without our subsidies. I make a point of never using any French when I'm here — not that I can remember much from school.'

If Gaffney was listening, he was hiding it well.

'And what about this, Staff? Why's Mills calling us back to HQ when we're in the middle of a surveillance detail? I don't like it.'

Gaffney shrugged, 'Dunno. He wants to see us, we go an' see him. Just get us there in one piece.'

Megan sighed, but said nothing.

They were shown straight into the superintendent's office. 'Staff Sergeant Gaffney, Constable Brown? I'm Donald Mills. I'm in charge of C Division Combined Forces, as you probably know. This is Lootenant Bauche, from the SPVQ. Sit down, please. It's a pleasure to have our Ontario colleagues aboard.'

Now Megan really was worried. Aboard what? Gaffney was supposed to be running an independent surveillance, reporting to his own Combined Forces superiors back in Ontario. It didn't sound good. Out the corner of her eye she noticed the city cop leering at her. She wasn't impressed. He was late thirties, with a shaved head, pockmarked cheeks, and teeth like a rodent. And he was French Canadian.

'I'll tell you right out, Staff, your team has been seconded to me effective immediately. Inspector Ames has been informed already. The good news is, it'll probably only be for twenty-four hours.'

Gaffney nodded, 'What about Beam, sir?'

Mills gestured towards Bauche, 'The SPVQ will be taking over until we wrap up Cable Car. That's why I wanted to see Constable Brown as well. I believe you made Beam originally?' he asked Megan.

'Yeah, sir. You're familiar with Godasse Monbourquette?'

'The Bandidos' armourer?'

'Yessir. We were watching him in Toronto. He had a very brief meeting with the man we've identified as John Beam. You can't miss him cos of the scar on his face. We followed him down here yesterday. So far all we know is that he entered the country from Ireland last Wednesday. He spent last night at the Hilton. At the moment he's in Battlefield Park, headed for the Citadel. We think he's going to meet someone — soon.'

'Another biker?'

'We don't know, sir.'

Mills nodded. 'Inspector Ames told me your initial work was excellent. He also said you're just waiting out your seven for promotion?'

'I hope so, sir,' she tried to sound modest.

'Glad to hear it.' He addressed Gaffney, 'To maintain continuity, I'm assigning Constable Brown to Lootenant Bauche's squad.'

Megan started a protest — thought better of it — and shut up.

'*Mademoiselle*, I look forward to our mutual liaison,' said Bauche.

Megan curled her lip in response.

'You'll report to Lootenant Bauche until your team takes over the surveillance again. Thank you, Lootenant,' said Mills.

'*Merci, monsieur*,' Bauche stood, and held the door open for Megan.

Megan took another look at him, and couldn't contain herself any longer — promotion or not. 'Sir, may I have a word in private?'

'No.'

Megan fumed as Bauche drove the Dodge Intrepid onto 9th Airport Street. 'Let's get a couple of things straight, Lootenant.'

'*Oui*, if you like,' he replied genially.

'First, it's not *mademoiselle*, it's 'officer' or 'constable'. Is that clear?'

'If you wish to remind me of your rank, I might observe that in the *Service de police de la Ville de Québec* constables show more courtesy to their officers than I have yet to see.'

The jerk couldn't even speak English properly. 'I don't give a damn about the SPVQ. You've got the highest unsolved homicide rate in the country. That tells me everything I need to know.'

'*No, no* — '

'Second, you can drop the Gallic charm, it's wasted on me. Then you can tell me what you know about Beam.'

'I assure you, *madem* — Officer — Brown, I have been fully briefed by your commandant. Even as we chat so amiably, my deputy is taking over from your Sergeant Gaffney's deputy. This man, Beam, he is no longer in the park. He is taking a tour around *La Citadelle*. There is nothing to be concerned about. A dozen of my best men are on this job. You will see, and you will be more respectful.'

Megan doubted it. She curled her lip again, and stared out the window.

Bauche muttered something in French, and shook his head. 'I had hoped for a more cordial *détente*,' he gave Megan another lascivious smile, but she was ignoring him. He took the opportunity to run his eyes over her dark blonde hair — tied back in a pony tail — her strong shoulders, and the curve of her breasts.

'*Pièce de résistance*,' he said to himself.

Fifteen minutes later they were still en route to the Citadel when Bauche's cell phone rang. He switched it to speaker and responded to the rapid-fire French in kind. After a minute or so he terminated the conversation with a *merde*.

'Well?' Megan asked.

'It seems you are not bilingual, Officer Brown. That is deplorable in a police agent, but luckily for you my English it is excellent, no?'

'No. Was it Beam?'

'*Oui*. Beam, he has left *La Citadelle*. He is now carrying a bag — a sporting bag — that he had not before.'

'Who gave it to him?'

'It was not seen. He was with a large tour group.'

Megan wasn't surprised. In addition to the city police's poor reputation, the provincial *Sûreté* had recently been rescued by the Mounties after they made a hash of the biker war between the Hell's Angels and the Bandidos. Three years on the gangs were still using Montreal as their base. So perhaps she shouldn't have been surprised when, only two hours after she'd last set eyes on Beam, Bauche's squad lost him somewhere in the Port of Quebec. She shouldn't have been surprised, but she was. Surprised and pissed.

Very pissed.

* * *

Charter skimmed through the dossier a second time, hoping he'd find something to make the job more palatable. He didn't. He'd killed three times before, always with good reason, never like this. He went through it again, but there was still nothing to justify the execution. The target had been selected because he was going to embarrass a government. That was it, nothing more. And it wasn't good enough for Charter. The target was also a cop. Charter didn't kill cops. Even after four years in the Secret Service, he still believed cops were the good guys. Maybe not every single one, but they deserved the benefit of the doubt. And there was no doubt about Jake

Rautenbach: all the evidence pointed to a good cop suffering from combat fatigue.

Born, Melmoth, KwaZulu-Natal, 1974. National Service, South African Medical Services, 1992. Selected for elite 7th Medical Battalion Group, 1994. Qualified Operator 5 Special Forces Brigade, 1996. Parents emigrated Canada, 1996. Commissioned, 1999. Resigned 2003, rank lieutenant. Operational deployments: Lesotho, 1998; Burundi, 2000.

There were seven more operational deployments, but no details. They were all classified above Charter's level.

Recruited by Royal Canadian Mounted Police direct for undercover work, 2003. Rank: constable; unit: Organised Crime Branch Undercover Operations. Operational deployments: infiltration of one of six Quebec chapters of the Hell's Angels; began August 2003, ongoing.

Within three months Rautenbach had begun providing his handlers with top quality intelligence. In January, they'd lost contact with him. In April, he disappeared: missing, presumed dead. Then, twelve days ago, he'd phoned the South African Embassy in Ottawa. He'd been on the run for two months and he wanted to come in, but he was a nervous wreck. He was completely unravelled and convinced that the Hell's Angles, the Bandidos, and his handlers all wanted him dead. Isolated and desperate, he'd reached out to the Secret Service intelligence officer that took the call. Cynthia Cele had quickly established a rapport with him and now she was the only person he trusted.

The problem, as far as Pretoria was concerned, was that he wanted to talk. He was prepared to give evidence in court against the Hell's Angels in exchange for a new identity, but he also wanted to talk to the SABC about his missions in Special Forces. The pressure of the last eight years had finally cracked him and he wanted to come clean about everything. It was a catharsis that was not going to be allowed to happen. If Charter hadn't found his own mission so repellent, he would've laughed at the irony. Rautenbach phoned the South African embassy because he didn't trust the Mounties, and in doing so, he'd sealed his fate. It wasn't the Mounties who wanted him dead, it was the South Africans.

He was coming in tomorrow, the second of July, on Charter's thirty-sixth birthday.

Charter looked down at the sports bag with the MacMillan TTR-50 sniper rifle inside. He wouldn't have the opportunity to test fire it, but it probably wouldn't matter. A couple of years ago in Afghanistan a Canadian soldier had used the same model to make the longest sniper kill in history at two thousand four hundred and thirty metres. Charter opened the curtains in his room at the Holiday Inn Select. The *Au couer de Saint-Roch* church towered above the plaza. Rautenbach would be at the entrance tomorrow at noon. It was fifty metres away, if that.

The scar on his cheek twisted into a scowl, contorting half his face with it.

* * *

Megan was exhausted. She'd spent most of the night helping Bauche and his keystone cops look for Beam. She'd been back on the job before breakfast, and she hadn't left Bauche's side all morning. It was the only way to make sure the dickhead put some effort in. But despite her efforts, and the extra men assigned to the job, Beam was nowhere to be found. Not only was Bauche incompetent and lazy, but he showed a complete lack of remorse or embarrassment. Ever slack, or what? Meanwhile Beam was probably long gone. Probably left Quebec City yesterday.

Lucky for some.

After nearly five fruitless hours with Bauche, she was beginning to enjoy riling him. 'Every single hotel?'

'*Oui, oui!* I have heard you the first time, Officer,' he gripped the steering wheel tight.

Sooner or later he was going to lose his temper. Megan hoped sooner. 'You've showed this photo to every reception in every hotel in this dump?'

'My men have done exactly that. I tell you again, I am in command. I give orders, and they are followed to the letter. I am rapidly tiring of your chastisement. It is irritating in the extreme.'

'What about the one we just passed?' Megan indicated over her shoulder, south on the *Rue de la Couronne*.

'*No*, not that one,' said Bauche, before lapsing into French. There was a problem with the traffic up ahead, and everything had ground to a halt.

'Take off! You haven't checked the Holiday Inn?'

'*No*, Officer, I have not, nor will I be checking it.'

'You damn well will! Turn around.'

'You are a most ignorant woman, are you not? All police have been ordered to stay away from Saint-Roch. It is where Operation Cable Car is taking place. How could you not know this?'

'Cos I've been too busy trying to find

the suspect you fucking lost!'

Bauche smiled, pleased to get a reaction. 'I know about this. In my position as lieutenant of criminal investigations, I know all that takes place in the *Ville de Québec*. And I know more than you, even though your Combined Forces is responsible for this operation.'

'I don't care about Operation Cable Car, I want to find Beam.'

'Ah, but you should care. Cable Car concerns an agent from your own force,' said Bauche as they inched forward.

'Fascinating. Now let me out. If you won't check the Holiday Inn, I will.'

'It is not permitted. In a few minutes, your force will secure their agent outside the *Au couer de Saint-Roch, l'église et la rue Saint-Joseph*. The Holiday Inn is situated next to *l'église*. We may not go there. All uniform and plainclothes police have been ordered to keep away. This agent is . . . how you say . . . excitable? They do not want him scared away from — '

'I don't care. Just stop. I'll keep a low profile, no one will know.'

'*No*, I will not. This is an operation of international significance. I will not disobey orders, and neither will you. Your colleague, he is from *Afrique du Sud* and there is an agent from their government working with the Combined Forces. It is all of the utmost importance.'

'Where did you say he's from?' asked Megan.

Traffic stopped again, and Bauche turned to her, '*Afrique du Sud* . . . er, Africa South?'

'South Africa. You realise Beam is South African?'

'And what of it?'

'And he's been in contact with Monbourquette. Monbourquette, the armourer.'

They started moving again. 'I do not see what you are meaning. The solution, it is simple. My men have contacted the hotel by telephone. Beam is not there.'

'Does the Holiday Inn overlook this church?'

'*Oui, oui*, it does.'

Megan gripped his arm, 'And it's the only hotel where you haven't shown this photo?'

'*Oui*, we have already discussed this matter. Let go of me, woman, I — '

Megan was out the car before he could finish. She heard a loud *putain* from the behind as she dodged a couple of cars to reach the pavement. She weaved her way through the pedestrians and broke into a jog. The Holiday Inn receptionists needed to see the photo, and they needed to see it now.

⋆ ⋆ ⋆

Charter scanned the plaza below. He'd paid for a late check-out, and already packed his luggage in the car. All except for the MacMillan. In addition to its awesome killing range, the rifle was a semi-automatic with a five round magazine. If something went wrong, he might get time for another shot. Might. The silencer would help, but in all likelihood Rautenbach — nervous wreck or not — would realise he was under fire and his training would take over. Not to mention the Mounties. If they were any good they'd have him covered and away in a matter of seconds. In which case it would most likely be just the one shot. He would have to make it count.

He checked his watch: five minutes to go.

No sign of Rautenbach or Cynthia yet. Charter had worked with Cynthia before, in London. She was an ex-cop from Gauteng, and he liked her. He doubted she knew anything about the execution or his mission. He wondered if she would've agreed to meet Rautenbach if she'd known she was being used to set him up. Probably not. Some people had managed to keep their integrity intact. Charter's scar twitched. He hadn't ever killed a cop before, and he didn't feel like starting on his birthday.

* * *

Megan ran into the Holiday Inn forecourt, barged her way through the queue, and flashed her identification card at the receptionist.

'*Bonjour madame. Je peux vous aider?*'

Did any Quebecker speak English? 'I'm

looking for this man,' she waved the photo of Beam, 'Have you seen him?' The receptionist looked about thirteen under his designer stubble. He took the photo and squinted at it.

Bauche appeared at her elbow, breathing heavily, '*Je suis agent de police du SPVQ. Vouz avez vu cet homme?*'

Come on, come on.

'*Il est ici à l'hôtel?*'

Yes or no? Either he's been here or he hasn't.

'*Euh . . . oui, monsieur l'agent . . .*'

Yes, what? Was he here?

'*Et où est-il en ce moment?*' asked Bauche.

'*C'est bien Monsieur Charter?*'

Bauche pointed at the photo, 'This is Mr Charter. He is here now!'

Charter? It must be him. No one could mistake that scar. Megan was thinking quickly: Beam was still in the hotel; the Mountie would be outside the church . . .

'*Il est dans la chambre six cent huit . . .*'

She charged off, 'Come on, Bauche! He's going to kill him. We gotta get him before he makes the hit!'

'I will take the stairs, you will take the elevator,' he shouted from behind.

Another one of Bauche's bright ideas. There were three elevators, so they'd be better off sticking together. Megan took the first one, punched number sixteen, and drew her Smith & Wesson. A guest was about to step in with her, but he saw the pistol and changed his mind. Bauche disappeared off to the right and the lift doors finally closed. She prayed there would be no stops.

* * *

Charter saw Cynthia mount the eleven steps to the semi-circular dais outside the church entrance. She stopped outside the first set of red doors and he took up the MacMillan. He rested it on the ironing board, the last three inches of the twenty-seven inch barrel protruding from the neat circular hole he'd cut in the window. He centred the sights on Cynthia. She was hard to miss in an orange skirt-suit that seemed all the brighter for her dark brown skin. An attractive woman, calm and poised, exactly as he remembered her. She walked slowly along the dais, as if admiring the architecture.

Charter took his eye from the sight: three minutes after twelve.

He used the bolt action to slide the first round into the chamber. The Macmillan used heavy calibre bullets, half an inch in diameter. The exit wound from a torso shot would be fatal, but Charter would aim for the head. Rautenbach's death might be undeserved, but it would at least be painless. He focused on Cynthia again, relaxed his shoulders and arms, and waited.

Thirty seconds later Rautenbach appeared.

* * *

Two, three, four, five . . .

Megan watched the numbers light up as the elevator climbed. How long was it going to take Bauche to run up sixteen floors? What was he thinking? Maybe if you got past the huge nose, bad skin, and buck teeth, he was a finely-tuned athlete. She doubted it.

Six, seven, eight, nine . . .

Chances were, she'd be on her own up there. She cocked a round into the chamber of the nine-mil, a compact model she was comfortable with.

Ten, eleven, twelve, thirteen . . .

She'd drawn her service pistol several times in the past six years, but never fired it in anger. Never shot to kill like her sister had. And her brother. He'd just gone out to Haiti with his regiment. He wouldn't hesitate — would she? She rested her right index finger on the trigger guard. Thanks to Bauche, she might just find out. She swallowed loudly, her mouth suddenly dry.

Fourteen, fifteen, sixteen . . . the elevator bumped to a halt.

Megan took a deep breath, moved her finger to the trigger, and flexed her knees. The door opened. She moved out quickly, weapon held low. *Six cent huit*. Room eight on the sixteenth floor. It was off to the right. She pointed the nine-mil at the door. No sign of Bauche. No time to wait.

Could she kill Beam if she had to?

No time for questions.

She moved up to the right-hand side of the door, side-on. Took a last breath. 'Police!' she fired twice at the lock, kicked the door open, and burst in —

It took her less than three seconds to realise she'd screwed up. *Six* was six, not sixteen. Fucking French, why couldn't they speak more slowly? She turned and sprinted for the stairs.

Bauche was on the sixth floor. Slumped against the wall of the stairwell, flailing at a Ka-Bar knife sticking out of his shoulder. His Beretta was lying on the floor next to him. He saw her and shouted something incomprehensible.

'Shut up! Where is he? Where's Beam!'

Bauche started gabbling again, waving downstairs. Megan took them three at a time. Down the stairs, into the lobby, out onto the *Rue de la Couronne*.

But Beam, Charter, or whoever the hell he was, was gone. And he had left a decapitated corpse lying sprawled outside the *Au couer de Saint-Roch, l'église et la rue Saint-Joseph*.

Fall Guy

The mission was simple: book in at the ski resort, find Brooks, shoot him. Then get on the next bus to Turin, and take the first flight back to Dublin. He should have been dead by Thursday at the latest. But he wasn't. Creek had held back because there were too many players on the field. He didn't know who they were. Mafia, spooks, undercover cops, other assassins? Whatever they were, they'd had plenty of opportunities to pick Creek up. He'd even left the Beretta in a sealed plastic bag in the toilet cistern on Wednesday. He couldn't think of anywhere more obvious. When he returned in the evening he could tell someone had been in the room. But the Beretta was still there. And two days later he was still on the slopes. So the spooks also wanted Brooks dead.

Creek was surprised he'd been given the mission. There'd been rumours of a purge for a few weeks now. The word was, everyone who'd been in the security forces prior to the 1994 elections was being retired. Police, Defence Force, Intelligence Agency, Secret Service — no one would escape this time. And Creek was old school. Only by a year or so, but that wouldn't make any difference. So when he'd received his third summons from the Director General's office, he'd assumed they were letting him go. But it was another job, a favour for the Americans this time. It seemed the new government needed reliable killers just as much as the old.

Creek realised he hadn't paid enough attention to the turn ahead.

The orange plastic safety netting loomed rapidly. He twisted into a parallel left turn, kicked up a flurry of snow, then hopped to his right, braking sharply. The deceleration was just enough to allow him to take the turn without ploughing through the netting into the trees beyond. Creek heaved a sigh of relief — straightened up — and found himself a metre away from a skier who'd stopped to take in the view. There was nothing he could do except save himself, so he crouched low and hit the man with his right shoulder. He heard a grunt, veered wildly, corrected himself, and skidded to a halt.

When he turned back to look, the man was gone.

Creek left the run, skiing down to the pine trees. A couple of metres into the wood, he saw the man lying on the snow. He must have bumped him off the slope. He'd only fallen a couple of metres down the bank, but Creek scissored his skis forward to give him a hand. The man was lying on his back, motionless. Creek wondered if he'd hit his head on one of the trees — then he saw who it was. First Sergeant Arnold T. Brooks, US 1st Special Forces Operational Detachment D. A veteran Delta Force Operator and a serial killer who'd notched up twenty-eight women in thirteen countries. And those were only the ones the CIA knew about. Creek stepped out of his skis, dropped his poles, and stamped his way through the last few metres of powdery snow.

Brooks groaned, and started to push

himself up into a sitting position.

Creek glanced up to the slope to make sure no one was there. Then he moved in behind Brooks, pulled his head back, and slit his throat with an Eickorn combat knife. Twenty-three years of covert operations and three wars didn't make the skin any tougher. Creek kept himself clear as the blood spurted out over the snow, and dropped the twitching body. The blood steamed in the cold air as flakes of snow began to fall.

Creek hurled the Eickorn further into the trees and returned to his skis. He had just enough time to get back to the Sporthotel, pick up his rucksack, and ski down to Cesara for the last bus at five. By the time they found Brooks, he'd be halfway to Turin. By the time they found he was missing, he'd be back at Alexandra House. Creek bent down to turn his skis around and heard someone on the slope above skidding to a halt.

Quickly, he picked up the poles and slotted his boots back into the skis. He heard a couple of men speaking Italian on the slope — no, they'd come down the bank into the wood — they were heading his way. The man in the lead and Creek saw each other at the same time. It was one of the spooks. Creek pointed his skis down slope, off-piste through the wood, and pushed himself forward. He saw the man draw a pistol. Creek crouched low, and winced in anticipation.

Crack!

The shot rang out behind and Creek heard the bullet thump into a tree trunk. Crack, Crack! More shots. He ducked even lower, weaved in between the trees, and careered wildly down the mountain. More shots — shouts — then shots again. Creek threw himself around a tree — was caught by a branch — regained his balance — and hurtled down towards the bottom of the valley.

Three minutes later.

Creek slowed and stopped, heart pounding and chest heaving. He listened for a full ten seconds. Nothing. The snow was falling thick and fast. It would cover his tracks. He swivelled to his left, so he was facing north, and moved off abreast of the river flowing far below. The spooks had been following him. It was the only way they could've found him so soon. And they weren't cops either. Cops identified themselves before they started shooting. They wanted Brooks and Creek dead. Two deaths: nice, neat, no questions asked.

Change of plan.

No going back to the hotel now. Creek had everything he needed on him: wallet, passports, compass, binoculars, map. He would stay off-piste until he passed below the Sporthotel — which should be coming up on the left shortly. Then he'd join the blue run down to Cesara Torinese. Once he was on that he knew it would take no more than twenty minutes to reach the bus stop. He checked his watch: sixteen twenty, plenty of time.

Sixteen thirty-one.

Creek still hadn't seen the Sporthotel, or found the blue run, but there was a helicopter circling overhead. Somehow he didn't think it was mountain rescue. He took out the binoculars and read the markings through the snow: *Arma dei Carabinieri*, Italy's paramilitary police.

They must've been on standby.
Did they have orders to shoot on sight?
The snowfall showed no signs of abating and Creek knew he was safe in the trees, but he was running out of time. He slid forward to the edge of the wood and turned the binoculars down the valley to the town below.
It was a trade-off now.
He could keep skiing north until he found a run to take him down to the town. But if he didn't find one in the next five minutes he'd miss the bus and be caught by the police. Alternately he could take a bearing on the road winding along next to the river below, and head straight for it. He'd have to ditch the skis because the ground was too uneven. It was less than three kilometres away, so he should reach it in time if he didn't twist an ankle or worse en route. But if he did fall — well, then it would be just the same as if he'd missed the bus. Creek ditched his skis and poles and set off at a jog.
Sixteen forty-four.
Creek was puffing and panting, fighting his way through the thick blanket of snow

on the ground, but he was making good time. The slope was steep, and gravity was doing most of the work. He just had to keep his balance, and keep watching where he put his feet. Less than a kilometre to go: nearly there.

Sixteen forty-nine.

Creek could see the river now, about fifty metres ahead. He forced himself on — stumbled — couldn't regain his footing, and tumbled head over heels. He went over once, twice — couldn't pull out of the fall — and pitched headlong. He bounced off a tree, hit the ground heavily, and rolled down slope on his side. He spun around and around until — thump — he stopped suddenly. The impact winded him and he felt pain shoot through his right thigh. He kept still and forced himself to breath deeply. Then he looked down: he'd rolled into a fallen tree, and the jagged edge of a cracked branch had impaled his right quadricep.

Creek froze.

He heard a voice — voices. Three men were walking up from the river. Wearing Alpine camouflage and balaclavas;

carrying rifles. Then a fourth. They were fanned out across to the south, walking up to Sagna Longa and the Sporthotel. Creek kept still as the heavy flakes fell on his face and covered his body. More voices — to the north this time. Another four cops sweeping up the slope to Sagna Longa. He shuddered at the pain, but forced himself to hold still. At least the wood sticking in his wound kept it from bleeding heavily.

Two deaths: nice, neat, no questions asked. Brooks, an operator discovered to have a penchant for torturing young women to death, no longer any use to Delta Force. Creek, an officer who knew too many secrets and had been around too long, no good to the South African Secret Service. No good alive. Welcome to the purge.

Sixteen fifty-nine.

When the men were out of earshot Creek tightened his abdominal muscles to keep his lower body still, and pulled off his jacket, sweatshirt, and thermal vest. He put the sweatshirt and jacket back on and tore the vest into three strips. He folded one of the strips into a small, thick square. Then he clenched his jaw tight and used his left hand to shove his leg off the spike. The blood gushed out and he clamped the makeshift bandage over it. He tied the other two strips tight around his thigh. Then he pushed himself to his feet, and put a little weight on the leg. It hurt like hell, but it would work.

Change of plan.

He dismissed the alternate escape route he'd been given. Everything from the Secret Service was part of the trap. Time to take the quickest route out of Italy on his own. He took out the map and compass. Claviere, on the border, was about six kilometres west-north-west; Montgenèvre, the closest French settlement, was a further two kilometres.

He dropped John Creek's passport in the snow and set off for Montgenèvre.

The Secret Agent

Penzance, Friday 10th June, 1522 hours

'You're sure no one can see us?'

Sommer looked up from the tripod-mounted Olympus and grimaced, 'I been doing this since you were a Brownie, an' all.'

'Sorry, I'm bein' a divvy,' said Jessica Smith. Then she exaggerated her normally lyrical Liverpudlian accent and added, 'They didn't have Brownies where I grew up. It wasn't tha' sorta neighbourhood.'

Sommer smiled, 'I can believe it.'

They were watching the entrance to the Admiral Benbow from a room above the Turk's Head, on the other side of Chapel Street. Jessica lifted her binoculars and peered through the gap in the net curtains. She didn't need to use them, but it was something to do to pass the time. She examined the life-size model of the smuggler on the roof, and then the picture of the admiral himself on the sign suspended above the entrance. 'They've been in there nearly three hours. Wha' the heck can they be doin'?' She turned as the door behind them opened.

'Any movement?' asked Detective Inspector Moon.

'Not yet,' Sommer shook his head.

Moon handed Sommer and Jessica a beaker of tea each, and checked his watch. 'What the fuck can they be doing?'

'You sure this geezer's the right man for the job, guv?' asked Sommer.

Moon frowned, 'Why?'

'He looked out of shape when we went to his gaff.'

Moon shrugged, 'Maybe. But he took the Yank out, didn't he. Practically cut his head off. And that was only three months ago.'

'Yeah, I s'pose,' Sommer didn't sound convinced.

'Besides, once he's in, I couldn't give a flying bat's fuck if he lives or dies. Just so long as he gives us what we want first.'

Sommer turned back to the window.

'Here we go!' He began shooting with the camera.

Moon pulled a monocular from his jacket and raised it to his eye. 'Pay attention, Jess. That's Penhelleck, their leader.'

A short, stocky man with brown hair came out the pub.

'Ex-marine,' said Jessica. 'He's done bird for armed robbery, ABH, and dealing; connected to organised crime in Bristol.'

'*Was*,' corrected Moon. 'He's set up on his own now. He was the Lizard bomber. Next up, our boy, Wilké.'

Another stocky man — with a long scar running down his left cheek — followed.

'His legend is dual citizen, retired major in the South African Army. Come back to the family home to make some money, but unemployed and lookin' for trouble. Tha' right, sir?'

'Exactly. Last one's Tregowan.'

A tall, muscular man with short black hair walked out behind Wilké.

'Also done time. All violent offences except a theft of motor vehicle. Suspected of killing the dealer in Perranuthnoe,' Jessica added.

'Right.'

The three men stood on the narrow pavement outside the pub. Penhelleck was speaking to Wilké. Sommer continued clicking away with the Olympus.

'Where's Connelly?' asked Jessica.

'He'll be back in Camborne. He's just the gofer; Penhelleck and Tregowan are the players.'

The two men turned away from Wilké, and walked past the Turk's Head towards St Mary's and the promenade. Wilké headed the other way.

'Let B an' H know India One an' Two are en route,' Sommer told Jessica.

She took her Airwaves handset from her belt.

'Forget it,' said Moon.

'Guv?' asked Sommer.

Wilké stopped outside a shop called Celtic Pine. He put his hands in his pockets, and examined the window display.

'No more surveillance once he's made contact. That's how we're playing this one.'

'You sure, guv?'

'Not negotiable, John. We're not gonna cock this up because we've been shown out.' Moon turned to Jessica, 'Leave it.'

She put the radio away. 'That means he's all on his own?'

'When you've been in the squad long enough to know Red Action from the White Wolves, you can open your mouth,' Moon snarled. 'Until then, shut it.' Jessica blushed under her freckles. 'What the fuck's he still doing outside the shop?'

'Probably giving us plenty of time to make him,' said Sommer. He turned to Jessica, 'That's the signal: if he walks past, it's off; if he goes in, we're in play.'

'Meanin' the Brigade have recruited him?'

'Yeah. *If* he goes in.' Sommer took the camera from the tripod. Moon put his monocular away.

'What does he think he's been recruited for?' asked Jessica.

'To let us know if the raid gets cancelled, and to make sure we don't have no civvy casualties,' said Sommer.

She nodded. It made perfect sense.

Wilké would have no reason to doubt them. She wondered if and when he'd realise he'd been lied to.

Down on the street, Wilké walked across the shop entrance to look at the second window.

'Come on, come on,' said Moon, 'What's it gonna be?'

Wilké hesitated a little while longer, then appeared to make up his mind, and marched into the shop.

'Game on!' Moon punched the air.

Taunton, Friday 24th June, 1058 hours

The armoured van indicated right, and slowed. Penhelleck handed a motorbike helmet to Wilké. Wilké slowed down, and quickly pulled the helmet over his head with one hand, while controlling the steering wheel with the other. The van crossed Heron Gate and stopped outside the National Westminster Bank. Penhelleck put his own helmet on, and watched the two in the back seat do the same as he secured Wilké's Velcro chinstrap. He waited for the first guard to debus, then said: 'Go.'

Wilké accelerated past the van, braked sharply, and pulled the Subaru Forester up across it. Tregowan and Connelly were out the vehicle before it stopped, both brandishing nine millimetre pistols. Penhelleck grabbed the shotgun from beside his seat and followed.

The first guard froze in panic. Then he opened his mouth to scream. Tregowan threw a left hook, caught him on the chin under his visor. There was a thud, a muffled grunt, and he crashed against the side of the van.

Connelly levelled his pistol at the driver's head, 'Get your fucking hands up!' He did, despite the bullet-proof glass.

Penhelleck pumped the Remington and pushed it into the driver's compartment. 'Take that helmet off. Now get out. This way, to me.' The driver shuffled along the seat and Penhelleck moved back to give him space.

Two people screamed and a car accelerated away.

Connelly moved round to the back of

the van. Wilké checked the road was clear, spun the Subaru around, and pulled up behind the van, so that he was facing the motorway.

When the driver climbed out he saw his colleague lying on his back, helmet off, with the muzzle of Tregowan's pistol between his teeth.

'If you want your friend to live, open the back, leave the funny money where it is, and hand over the cash. All of it. We been watching you all day.'

The driver stared down the barrel of the shotgun, nodding frantically. 'OK, OK, yeah . . . I'll do it, I'll do it. I need to get the key from him,' he pointed at the other guard. Tregowan stood up, and put his foot on the guard's neck. The driver removed the key and chain from his colleague's belt and hurried to the back of the van. As he turned to open it he saw Tregowan had resumed his position, and put the pistol back in the man's mouth.

Wilké pulled up the handbrake, put the Subaru in neutral, and ran to the back to open the boot. The driver handed the first metal box over to him and he stashed it at the rear. Then the next, and the next, until all five were stacked. He closed the boot, and climbed back in the car.

'Come on, fucking move it!' shouted Penhelleck.

'That's all — that's it.'

'What about them two!' Connelly shoved him further into the van.

'Dummies! They're dummies, I swear it! They're fitted with dye. They'll spray — '

'Shut your gob! Keys for the boxes — now!'

The driver waved a bunch of keys at Penhelleck. 'On there — they're on there.' Connelly grabbed them from him.

Penhelleck stared at the guard: 'You know who we are?'

He shook his head in terror, 'N . . . no, no! I don't know nothing.'

'You do now. We're the Kernow Republic Brigade. That's Kernow, as in Cornwall. Got it?' Before he could answer, Penhelleck smacked the side of the shotgun into his temple. The guard's head snapped back and he collapsed onto the road. 'Come on, boys!'

Connelly was first in the Subaru, sliding in behind Wilké. Then Penhelleck, who kept the Remington on his lap. Tregowan was busy kicking the guard in the head.

'Come on, Andy!' Penhelleck shouted. Then to Wilké: 'Go!'

Wilké waited a couple of seconds before flooring the accelerator. The Subaru hurtled off as Tregowan tumbled in. Wilké dodged a car in front, veered onto the right-hand side of the road, and had them the first roundabout less than half a minute later. He slowed down, and eased into the clockwise flow of traffic.

'Ready?' asked Penhelleck.

'*Ja*.'

Penhelleck undid the chinstrap, waited for Wilké to duck his head, and pulled the helmet off. 'Nice work. Keep it tidy, Wilké, keep it tidy.' Wilké indicated left at the next roundabout, drove past a Travelodge, and turned into a crowded Sainsbury's parking lot. 'Know what you're doing, Andy?'

'Yeah. How many boxes you want me to take?'

'Three.'

'Right. Load the three boxes into the Skoda, take the motorway down to Exeter. Sort the cash on the way, ditch the boxes. Make sure the alibi's looking good, and I'll meet you back at the base tomorrow, yeah?'

'Yeah. You might have to sit tight for a coupla days. I'm not sure how long I — me and Wilké — are gonna be.' Wilké parked two cars down from two silver cars, a Skoda and a BMW. 'Check the keys first. Leave me the two I need. I can't be arsed with breaking into these things.'

Tregowan backed the Skoda out while Connelly opened the Subaru's boot. They transferred three of the boxes to the Skoda while Penhelleck cleared the shotgun. Wilké kept his eye on the surrounds, but no one was taking much notice of them. Tregowan and Connelly were careful not to rush, and there was nothing except for the unusual shape of the metal boxes to alert anyone to the crime still in progress. Penhelleck put the Remington into a bag, and Connelly dropped two keys in Wilké's lap.

'We're off.'

'I'll ring you tomorrow,' said Penhelleck.

Tregowan and Connelly left and Wilké opened the BMW with his key fob. He and Penhelleck took a box each, locked the Subaru, and put the swag in the BMW boot. Penhelleck slung the bag with the Remington in the front, and Wilké started the car. 'Where to?'

'Back onto Toneway, then north onto the motorway.'

'North?'

'Yeah. Next junction is twenty-four. Go off there and take the A38 for Minehead.' Penhelleck followed Wilké's example and clipped his seatbelt in.

'Why there?' Wilké turned out the car park.

'Cos that's what I said.' When Wilké was silent, Penhelleck continued, 'We're meeting a mate of mine,' he stopped as they heard a siren and saw a police car flying towards the bank.

'Let's hope they keep going the wrong way, or we might havta test these driving skills of yours. Tell me, how does a squaddie get trained as a getaway driver?'

Wilké joined the traffic headed for Bristol. 'I did some VIP protection training. Part of it was a two week advanced driving course run by the cops.'

'You said you were in the infantry.'

'I was.'

'Perk of the job being a fucking Rupert, was it?'

'Rupert?'

'An officer.'

'Something like that.'

'You reckon you could outrun any coppers that give us trouble, or will I have to use this?' he pointed at the bag.

'In this car, *ja*.'

Penhelleck nodded. 'We'll see. Just keep it tidy. We should be turning off in about seven or eight minutes.'

'When do you want to get rid of the boxes?'

'No rush. Wait until we get to the national park. I know a few places where we can do the deed without getting clocked. Then we're off to meet my mate.'

Half an hour later Penhelleck told Wilké to take the turn for Dunster. They passed through the village then turned off on a narrow lane signposted for Wootton Courtenay. Wilké didn't know where they were, and he didn't like the idea of being alone with Penhelleck in a remote part of the countryside. Following instructions again, he turned down a dirt track, and stopped next to a small grove of trees. There was no one in sight: no buildings, no vehicles, no animals, and no people.

Not a stitch.

'Right, let's see what we got.'

Both boxes were full of notes, most of them twenties. Penhelleck took another bag from the boot and counted the bundles of cash as he threw them in. 'Twenty grand in each. Forty for us and maybe sixty for Andy. Hundred grand the lot. Nice work if you can get it.' He stuck a wad of notes in his pocket.

'What about these?' Wilké indicated the empty boxes.

'We'll wipe them down first. Then sling them in the trees over there.'

When Wilké returned, Penhelleck was leaning against the boot with his arms folded. He had an HS95 nine millimetre in his right hand. Wilké knew the make because he'd used one before. He felt the bulge of his own .357 revolver under his belt. It wasn't reassuring, because there was no way he could get to it before Penhelleck fired. If Penhelleck fired. Wilké swallowed hard, and tried not to show his fear.

'Well, my foreign friend, there's just one more thing.'

The scar on Wilké's left cheek twitched, but he held Penhelleck's gaze, '*Ja*?'

'When I recruited you to the Brigade I told you we needed a fourth man for a big job. You thought this was it, didn't you?'

He had assumed nothing of the sort, but replied in the affirmative.

'Wrong. This was a little test for you, but you haven't passed . . . '

Wilké was running through his options rapidly, weighing up distances and estimating his chances of survival. He remained silent.

'Not yet, anyway. I need your shooter.' Penhelleck pushed off from the car, pointed the HS95 at Wilké, and beckoned him closer with his left hand. 'Lift your shirt for me so I don't have to go touching your nuts, will you?'

Wilké advanced, stopped an arm's length away from Penhelleck, and slowly raised his shirt. This would be the time to strike.

Penhelleck turned slightly to one side and grabbed the rubber grip of the Manurhin revolver from Wilké's belt.

Wilké didn't move.

Penhelleck stepped back, a firearm in each hand. 'Good. You just passed the test. My mate, you see, he's not very trusting, and he knows you're a new boy. I promised him you'd be unarmed. Open the boot for me, will you?'

Wilké did as asked, then sat in the driver's seat.

Penhelleck unloaded the revolver, put the weapon and the loose rounds into the bag with the shotgun, and put the bag in the boot. Then he joined Wilké. 'Here's some pocket money until we get back to Redruth.' He gave him twenty twenty-pound notes. 'Now, can you find your way back to the A39?'

'I think so.'

'Good, let's go.'

'Who is this friend of yours?' Wilké asked as he steered the car in the direction he guessed was east.

'Name's O'Donoghue. An Irish fellah.'

Milton Keynes, Wednesday 6th July, 0842 hours

Moon and Sommer were sitting in an unmarked Astra, on a farm road about a mile from Junction 13 of the M1. Detective Chief Inspector Johnson spoke from the backseat, 'Right, run through it again for me.'

Moon checked his watch for the second time in less than a minute. 'John.'

'Okay, guv, we got Papa Charlie Two an' Four standing by at the roundabout at the entrance to the motorway. The rest of our firm, Three an' Five, are standing by off the Groveway roundabout to the north. Half the Blue Team of CO19 are in Range Rovers north an' south of us, outta sight. There's a spotter chopper in the air, also outta sight. The other half of the Blue

Team are standing by in a transport chopper at the local factory, with a second transport ready to pick us up if we scramble 'em. RAF Uxbridge an' Brampton have their radar stations on the alert, an' RAF Cottesmore is ready to put a couple Harriers in the air if there's any bother. An' we got radio contact with the prison van.'

Johnson did not look happy.

Moon checked his watch again, and spoke to Sommer, 'Does everyone know what they're supposed to be doing, John?'

'Yeah, we're all sussed, guv. A rabbit with trainers couldn't get through.'

'The briefing was good,' said Johnson, 'Now let's hope the plan works. For both our sakes,' he glared at Moon.

Moon tried to sound confident, 'Yeah, Harold, I appreciate the autonomy you've given me on this one. I won't let you down.'

The radio crackled, 'Control, Whisky Mike Ten.'

'Whisky Mike Ten, send.'

'Control, we are leaving Woodhill prison, over.'

'Received, Whisky Mike Ten. Papa Charlie One, Control.'

Moon keyed the mike, 'Papa Charlie One.'

'Papa Charlie One, did you copy last, over?'

'Affirmative, over.'

'Papa Charlie One, you have control of the net. Good luck. Out.'

'Papa Charlie One to all units, I have control. Whisky Mike Ten has left Woodhill. All units stand by. Radio silence until you have the eyeball.' Moon turned back to Johnson, 'Even if they don't spring the break here, we're still on top of them.'

'Better for us if they do it before the motorway.'

'Yeah, I know.'

'They will,' put in Sommer. 'It's too risky on the motorway — an' afterwards the van'll be stuck in London traffic. No, it has to be here.'

'You're right, John. I just hope Dave's covered every contingency. Otherwise there'll be hell to pay.'

'Papa Charlie One, Alpha Whisky Eight.'

Moon recognised the spotter chopper's call sign. 'Alpha Whisky Eight, send.'

'I have the eyeball: Whisky Mike Ten approaching Groveway roundabout, over.'

'Received.' Moon released the mike, 'I hope that fucking chopper stays out of sight. That's all we bloody need.'

'Papa Charlie One, Papa Charlie Three.'

'Papa Charlie Three, send.'

'I have the eyeball: Whisky Mike Ten is heading for your location, over.'

'Received.'

Two and a half minutes later Moon saw the prison van pass them. He gave it fifteen seconds, then told Sommer to follow. Sommer pulled out onto the arterial road.

'Papa Charlie One, Alpha Whisky Eight!'

'Alpha Whisky Eight, send!'

'Contact, contact! South of your position, over.'

'Papa Charlie one to all units: stand off. I say again: stand off from the contact . . . ' Sommer slowed down. ' . . . Alpha Whisky Eight, relay commentary in bursts, over.'

'Two BMWs, four suspects. Suspects

have rifles and are wearing motorbike helmets and flak jackets . . . the navigator is on the deck, driver is opening the van . . . Three prison officers on the deck . . . Eyeball on Zulu Two . . . '

Moon heard gunfire, 'What the fuck was that!'

'India Three fired a warning shot, no injuries. I repeat: no injuries . . . A chopper! Papa Charlie One, there is a bandit in the air . . . A white Sikorsky S-76.'

'Back to the RV, John.' Sommer turned the Astra around, heading back for the farm. Moon keyed the mike, 'Control, Papa Charlie One.'

'Papa Charlie One, send.'

'Initiate Operation Tombola.'

'Received, Papa Charlie One; initiating Operation Tombola, over.'

'Alpha Whisky Eight, sitrep?'

'Bandit has landed. Zulus boarding now . . . all Zulus and Indias aboard . . . bandit is taking off. I am standing off from bandit, over.'

'Control, Papa Charlie One.'

'Papa Charlie One, send.'

'Confirm RAF Uxbridge and Brampton have activated radar, over.'

'That's affirmative. Uxbridge are tracking bandit . . . stand by one. Bandit is heading south, south-west for Toddington. Alpha Whisky Eight Two, confirm you are en route to Papa Charlie One's location.'

'One mike, over.'

'That's the transport chopper coming for us,' said Moon to Johnson.

'Papa Charlie One, are you standing by for uplift, over?'

'Affirmative.' They were back on the farm road, and Moon saw two Range Rovers bouncing over the field towards them. 'Papa Charlie One and Blue Team standing by, over.'

The Eurocopter transport was ten seconds late to the rendezvous. As soon as it touched down, Moon, Sommer, Johnson, and six Specialist Firearms Command officers boarded.

Moon plugged his earphones in, and used his handset to call as the chopper took off. 'Control, Papa Charlie One.'

'Papa Charlie One, send.'

'I am airborne with the remainder of Blue Team; require sitrep from Uxbridge.'

'Uxbridge confirm bandit is still heading to Toddington, over.'

'Received. All Alpha Whiskys to assume position for air cordon.' The chopper climbed as the pilot estimated his position in relation to the other two aircraft. 'As soon as this is done we're sorted,' Moon told Johnson.

'Papa Charlie One, Control!'

'Send.'

'Uxbridge inform bandit has landed; I say again: bandit has landed . . . location: Houghton Regis, Dunstable.'

'Alpha Whisky Eight, Papa Charlie One. Did you copy last, over?'

'Affirmative. ETA half a mike, over.'

'Received, resume commentary when you have the eyeball.'

Johnson looked at Moon, 'Why has he landed already? We're barely off the ground.'

'Papa Charlie One, Alpha Whisky Eight.'

'Go!'

'I have the eyeball. Bandit has landed

. . . location, a field on the south side of Thorn. Repeat: Thorn . . . no eyeball suspects . . . heavy tree cover . . . Alpha Whiskey Eight One is landing.'

'What the hell is going on!' demanded Johnson.

'The spotter can't see the suspects. Don't worry, CO19 are landing.'

'I can bloody hear that,' Johnson said through grit teeth. He tapped the pilot on the shoulder and shouted, 'How long?' The man held up three fingers.

'Alpha Whisky Eight, stand off from bandit. Keep watch for any vehicles leaving the scene.' So long as the spotter chopper could identify the vehicles the suspects were in, the operation was still on.

'Alpha Whisky Eight, copied . . . Blue Team deploying . . . '

'Suspects, Alpha Whisky Eight, any suspects!' Moon shrieked.

'Negative, negative.'

'What the hell is going on!' Johnson repeated himself. 'Why can't they bloody see anything?'

Moon swore. Sommer looked wistful.

'Papa Charlie One, Blue Leader.'

'Blue Leader, send!' Moon gripped his radio as if it were a lifeline — and it was.

'Bandit is empty. My team are searching the farmhouse, but it appears Zulus have left in two vehicles, descriptions unknown . . . do you copy, Papa Charlie One?'

Moon did copy. He could now see the two choppers in the field below, as well as a small wood and an avenue leading to an arterial road. No vehicles had been seen leaving: the tree cover was too heavy.

Twenty miles away, Jessica was in the passenger seat of another unmarked car, flying south along the motorway.

'What happened?' asked DC Mastveer.

'I don't know, Sam. I think they used the chopper to take them just out of range of our cars, and then landed straight away.'

'What for?'

'Somehow they must have guessed we'd have a helicopter ready. So they landed before we could get the air cordon se' up. Now they're back in cars — only we don't know which ones.'

‘You mean John’s rabbit with trainers has left the building?’

‘More like they left us holdin’ the rabbit while they screw it.’

Despite himself, Mastveer smiled, ‘You have such a way with words, Jess. But I wouldn’t mention rabbits — or any small animal — when we meet up with Dave. He doesn’t like your sense of humour at the best of times.’

‘He doesn’t like *me* at the best of times. And don’t worry, I’ll be keeping my trap shu’.’

‘Look on the bright side,’ said Mastveer, ‘he might already be out of a job by the time we get there.’

Toddington, Wednesday 6th July, 0908 hours

Wilké drove the GSI onto the M1 northbound. Tregowan was next to him up front, and O’Donoghue directly behind him. O’Donoghue had been the navigator in the getaway chopper. The pilot had left Thorn on foot on his own, and Penhelleck had taken Connelly and Macnamara — the released prisoner — in another car, using a different route. Wilké wondered if there were police cars coming the other way down the motorway, from Milton Keynes. Probably. He also wondered what the hell he and the Kernow Republic Brigade were still doing at large.

'We're headed for Birmingham. The M6 — but no toll road — aye?'

'No problem.'

O'Donoghue was from Belfast, his accent thick. And there was also no mistaking he was in command. He always had been. Penhelleck had deferred to him before, in Devon, despite the fact that he'd arrived alone and never mentioned being part of any organisation. And he was keeping everything strictly need to know. Probably only he and Penhelleck knew their destination. Wilké didn't. O'Donoghue and Tregowan both carried sidearms — Berettas, they looked like — but Wilké was unarmed again. There were three assault rifles in the boot, two M4s and an M16, but he'd never make it to them in time if he needed to.

Where the hell was Moon?

Everything had gone according to plan: the raid had taken place as expected, and no prison officers had even been wounded, let alone killed. Moon had been right. As a foreigner, Wilké had escaped suspicion as a Special Branch agent. The initial meeting and introduction had been in his lodgings in Marazion, and then the offer of employment at the Admiral Benbow. Penhelleck couldn't pass up the opportunity of the disgruntled Major John Wilké, of Cornish descent, looking for a new war to fight. Wilké wasn't in the inner circle, but then neither was Connelly. Connelly was a skinny youth from Camborne and it was obvious that Penhelleck and Tregowan regarded him as a weak link. Since O'Donoghue had appeared on the scene, neither Connelly nor Wilké had been allowed anywhere on their own. And Penhelleck had only given them a detailed briefing first thing this morning. He'd left nothing to chance and it appeared his careful planning had worked.

Too well.

Tregowan switched the radio on.

'Watcher do that for?' asked O'Donoghue.

'Listen for traffic announcements. Don't wanna get caught up in a jam, do we, mate?'

'Switch it off. We got all the time in the world.'

Tregowan did as he was told.

The silence gave Wilké more time to think. He needed to think. Moon's instructions had been simple. The police commandos would strike as soon as the terrorists had Macnamara out of the prison van. Wilké was to throw down his weapon and keep low until the arrests were made. He would be taken along with the others, and then Moon and Sommer would separate him from the criminals. But there'd been no arrests, no police commandos, and no Moon or Sommer.

Wilké had assumed the man he'd helped escape was Connor Macnamara, the Real IRA commander responsible for bombing Birmingham city centre in November 2001. Wilké had been with the FBI at the time, and he recalled the bulletin because it stood out at a time when Moslem extremists completely dominated the Most Wanted lists. Macnamara was supposed to have fled to Southern Colombia, where he was sharing his bomb building skills with FARC revolutionaries in exchange for sanctuary.

Two years later, still with the FBI, Wilké recalled a Macnamara being arrested in London for importing and dealing cocaine. He'd assumed that the two were one and the same, until he'd heard Penhelleck call Macnamara 'Padraig' in the chopper. It was only then that Wilké realised Connor was still at large, and that it was his brother who'd been arrested in London. O'Donoghue was obviously RIRA, and he'd recruited Penhelleck and his Brigade to rescue Macnamara junior. Penhelleck had described it as assisting their Celtic brothers in arms. Big brothers in arms, more like.

None of which accounted for Moon's absence.

It was just after ten when Wilké took them onto the M6.

'Good lad,' said O'Donoghue, 'Now keep goin' 'til we get ter Cannock. Then take the A5 west. Should be signed for Shrewsbury, aye?'

'*Ja*,' Wilké replied. They all lapsed into silence again.

Traffic was surprisingly light and it was less than an hour later when O'Donoghue ordered Wilké to pull up at a Texaco garage. Once he'd refuelled, O'Donoghue told him to park up outside the Bell, and the three of them went in for lunch. O'Donoghue bought himself and Tregowan a Guinness each. 'None for you, son, you're designated driver. Watcher want?'

'Coffee, please.' Wilké thought about going to the toilet, and escaping out the window, but he didn't think they'd let him go alone. Not now, not yet. And, if he was honest with himself, he didn't want to leave just yet. He didn't like leaving a job half-finished. Even if he couldn't stand Moon, and even if Special Branch hadn't been honest with him. After the drinks came, he tried a straight question, 'Where are we going,

Mr O'Donoghue?'

'Listen — ' Tregowan spat, but O'Donoghue interrupted him.

'Don't soldiers in South Africa follow orders, now?'

'I've been following orders ever since Andy and Marc turned up at my digs.'

O'Donoghue leaned close, and Wilké could smell his sour breath. 'I like yer, Wilksey, yer handled yerself well today, and yer cold as ice. I like that in a man.' Wilké said nothing. 'And yera quiet fella. That's good for a soldier. Yer gonna get on well with your Brigade, yer are. I like a quiet man . . . like John Wayne . . . a quiet man . . . ' he laughed at his own joke, 'so I'm gonna tell yer where we're goin'. We're goin' to Plas Gwynant, a little village below Mount Snowdon.'

Wilké thought it made sense. Wales was the nearest Celtic homeland from Milton Keynes. He wondered if there were a group of local cranks in Snowdonia as well.

'That's right, Cornishmen, we're off to have a holiday in Cymru. A little place called Keeper's Cottage, above Llyn Dinas, right in the heart of the National

Park. We'll be there in three hours or so, and we'll be stayin' there 'til the heat dies down. But first we're gonna change vehicles in Shrewsbury, and pick up somethin' more suitable, aye?'

'What about Marc and Andy?' asked Tregowan.

'They're on their way too, with Padraig. We're just takin' different routes to be safe. It's been a crackin' job so far, well done ter both of yer. Especially since this job's gratis. But don't worry yerselves, there'll be plenty ter come yer way if yer keep up the good work,' he smiled knowingly, and sank a third of his pint on one large gulp.

Two hours after lunch, Wilké was driving a green Range Rover towards Llangollen. Tourist information signs informed him that he was not only on an historic coaching route, but also very close to what looked liked a Dalek museum. Wilké smiled to himself. Not because the Dalek and the Welsh dragon were such a strange combination — which they were — but because he considered his situation had improved since lunch.

Dramatically.

First, he'd eaten well, which was always good before action. Second, he now knew where he was going, and that he had about an hour and a half left to get there. Third, the morning's excitement and the lunch-time drinking had put Tregowan to sleep, and he was snoring away on the back seat. Fourth, O'Donoghue — although alert as ever — hadn't engaged his seatbelt. Neither had Tregowan. All Wilké had to do was drive into one of the many trees that lined their route, and he could be away with ease. He could've escaped right then, but he chose not to. Because he'd realised that Connor Macnamara would be waiting at Keeper's Cottage, and that Special Branch were relying on him to lead them there. Even if they hadn't had the courtesy to tell him, and even if he'd had to work it out on his own. Wilké disliked Moon, but he disliked terrorists more.

And he didn't like leaving unfinished business.

London, Thursday 7th July, 1127 hours

'Dave, Jack, get in here!' Johnson shouted across the squadroom. Moon followed DI Eyles in. 'Close the door and sit.' Johnson's landline was ringing and he unplugged the lead from the back.

'What the hell's happening?' asked Eyles.

'It appears six bombs were detonated on the Underground at ten to nine, all within a minute of one another. An hour later another bomb blew up a bus. SO13 are down there now.'

'Christ. Where?' asked Eyles.

'Liverpool Street, Edgware Road, and King's Cross St Pancras are the only ones confirmed for the Underground. The bus was in Tavistock Square.'

'How many — '

Moon cut Eyles off: 'Who?'

'No one's claimed responsibility yet, but we think *al-Qaeda*. Either *al-Qaeda* or *Hizb uh-Tihrir*. It looks strongly like suicide bombers, but that hasn't been released to the media. Unless we're completely incompetent, we think this lot are home-grown, and cleanskins. They'd better be cleanskins, or we're all in for the high jump. Regardless, C Squad is on it. All leave cancelled. Call in everyone at home, even if they're sick. No one goes off duty until I get the word from Lynda — '

'What — '

'Hold it, Dave! Jack, get moving. You'll be running your team as well as DS Byrne and five of Dave's DCs. Dave can keep Mastveer, Breach, Hedges, and Smith. Get the rest together and I'll issue actions in a minute.'

'Yes, sir,' Eyles left quickly.

'But — '

'Save it,' Johnson put his palm out. 'That's all you're getting, Sommer and four DCs.'

Moon's pale cheeks coloured, 'What! I'm supposed to track down one of Ireland's hardest with five men?'

'Don't take that tone with me! If you hadn't lost them in the first place, you wouldn't have to be tracking them down.' Johnson's temper rose, 'I gave you the autonomy you wanted, and look what bloody happened! Have you any idea how costly yesterday was? And I'm not just talking about the two bloody Eurocopters, either. When I took Operation Rogue to Lynda she said too expensive and too risky. But I talked her into it, more fool me. CO19, Thames Valley, NCIS, the RAF, the Prison Service . . . need I go on?'

Moon threw his hands in the air, 'Jesus fucking Christ! You may as well take me off Rogue as well, cos I can not find Macnamara with what you've left me.'

'No, I'm not taking you off,' Johnson jabbed a finger at him, 'Rogue is your baby, your cock-up, and you will finish the job to the best of your ability. Understood?'

'Yeah,' Moon mumbled.

'What about your agent?'

'What about him?'

'What more do you need? As soon as he gets in touch, use the local force for back-up. I'll make sure their Special Branch and firearms teams are on board.'

'That's not good — '

Johnson stood and leant over the desk.

He was a tall, broad man, physically imposing. 'This interview is finished,' he pointed at his door, 'Get out and get on with your work, or get out and post me your resignation. Your choice.'

Moon stood, scowled, and stormed out into the squadroom. He slammed his office door behind him and threw himself in his chair. He fished his mobile from his pocket and pushed a speed dial button.

'Sommer.'

'John, where are you?'

'Church.'

'Church!'

'Yeah, St John's in Cirencester. I'm with someone. What's goin' on in the Smoke? The Beeb are making it sound like the Blitz.'

'Not sure yet. Looks like seven bombs, *al-Qaeda*. Never mind that. Harry's taken half the fucking team off me. There's only you, B and H, Sam, and Jess left. Tell me you've got something,' Moon pleaded.

'Yeah, I might.'

'What?'

'Some geezers calling themselves Cymru Cyntaf. Means 'Wales First', or summing like that. Sorta like our Brigade boys; operate from Wrexham.'

'Yeah, they were involved with the riots a couple of years back, weren't they?'

'Yeah, that's them.'

'Connection?'

'Might be, but nothing concrete so far.'

'Never mind, so long as there's something — anything — to work on. Ring Sam and B and H. Get them to meet us at Wrexham nick. I'll get hold of the North Wales Special Branch, pick up Jess, and see you there.' Moon closed the phone and reached for his police directory.

Plas Gwynant, Tuesday 12th July, 0935 hours

By Saturday morning Wilké was sure Moon wasn't coming. He'd first expected a strike on Wednesday night, then in the early hours of Thursday or Friday morning. But when it hadn't happened by the time he woke up on Saturday, he knew that — this time — something really had gone wrong. As soon as he'd met Connor Macnamara and the other RIRA man, Mullen, he'd confirmed his suspicions about Moon's deception. The real reason Special Branch had coerced his employ was to lead them to Connor. The Brigade were supposed to escape with Macnamara junior. It had all been part of the plan.

But that plan had failed.

So Wilké had begun hatching his own plan. But in the three days since, he and Connelly were kept under constant supervision, and he'd had no opportunity to escape. In addition, none of the cell phones had any reception, and there was no landline in the four bedroom bungalow above Llyn Dinas. On the upside, they'd at least given him a pistol when he'd taken his turn on guard duty. He had it now — a Beretta nine millimetre — tucked under his belt. Also, his cover was holding, and he knew he could escape from the Brigade as soon as they returned home.

But he didn't want to let Connor Macnamara get away.

Connor addressed the seven of them, all gathered in the living room. 'Right fellas, yer all know what we're doin' now, don't yer . . . '

Wilké had thought about killing Penhelleck, when the two of them were together on stag, but it wouldn't have worked. Penhelleck was a tough customer, and always armed. Wilké would've had to shoot him to make sure, and without a silencer it would've alerted the rest. By the time he'd made his own escape, found the local police, explained the situation, and returned with them, the terrorists would've been long gone. It was no good.

'Padraig and I are takin' Caeghel down t' Beddgelert, where he'll find a bus. The rest of you are goin' with Michael to Capel-Curig. Drop him off there, and he'll get on the bus as well . . . '

If Wilké stayed with the Brigade, he'd end up losing Connor and the RIRA men. Perhaps he could alert the police that they would be on the ferry, but how? He'd be stuck in a Range Rover with three armed gangsters until Penhelleck decided he could clear off. The terrorists might be long gone by then. That wasn't any good either.

'We'll all make for Holyhead and the eleven-thirty ferry to Dublin. Us in the Rover and Caeghel and Michael on foot — separately, mind. Remember, the dozy coppers are gonna be out and about lookin' hard at passengers. But the good news is, they're all chasin' camel jockeys right now. So keep your cool and we'll be over before you know it. You boys know where to meet in Dublin. As for the Brigade . . . '

Wilké had been stuck with seven terrorists for five days and there'd been absolutely nothing he could do about it.

' . . . You gents'll be takin' yourselves and the armoury back to Kernow. It's been a pleasure to work with you, and I look forward to future joint operations. Is everythin' packed and ready, aye?'

Wilké had one — and only one — opportunity to stop them all. Right now.

Connor dismissed the men and everyone made last minute preparations for the journey.

'Have you packed the rifles?' Penhelleck called to Wilké.

'*Ja*, just put your bags in and we're good to go.'

'Top man, Wilké.'

Wilké had been designated to drive again, which suited him perfectly. The green Range Rover was sitting in the courtyard, doors and boot open, ready to leave. The Macnamaras climbed into the black one and started the engine. Connor shouted for Mullen, and he jogged out the cottage and joined them. Connor waved at O'Donoghue and Wilké as he drove off. Penhelleck, Connelly, and Tregowan appeared in the courtyard, and they all climbed in. Wilké started the engine.

Then switched it off.

'What?' asked Penhelleck, sitting next to him in the front.

'Sorry guys, I need a piss before I start.'

'Well, fucking hurry up.'

Wilké obliged, trotting around the side of the cottage. As soon as he was out of sight, he made for a metal bin full of firewood. He opened the lid and pulled out an M16 with two thirty-round magazines, the first taped to the second for a quick changeover. He thumbed the selector switch to automatic, and returned the same way he'd come. He stopped and looked around the corner of the cottage. The Range Rover was just over ten metres away. When he stepped out of cover he would be behind it and slightly to the right hand side. Perfect. He forced himself to take a deep breath.

Slowly in, slowly out.

Wilké took two steps into the courtyard, raised the rifle, and fired a two second burst into the Range Rover.

The crack of the gunfire echoed off the mountain slope above.

He took a long step to his right, and fired a second burst.

Glass, metal, flesh, and bone shattered as the bullets tore through them. Blood spattered against the windows. Wilké saw a silver flash from the backseat — a pistol pointed at him.

Another two second burst, another step to the right.

All the windows were splintered and

bloody: he couldn't see inside anymore.

Another burst — click.

Wilké fought to keep control. He unclipped the first magazine, clipped the second in, ripped the slide back, hefted the rifle to his shoulder, and advanced. He put two more bursts into the vehicle. He thumbed the selector switch to single shot, and opened the rear passenger door with his left hand.

Tregowan and Penhelleck were groaning, the other two still.

Wilké put a single round in each of the four heads, including Connelly, who didn't have much skull left.

The vehicle was wrecked, so Wilké left it, sprinting through the gate to the track to Plas Gwynant. He saw the other Range Rover winding its way down past the lake. The village was only a third of a mile away, but the distance by road was three times that. The Rover was about two hundred metres from his position. He knew the maximum effective range of the M16 was four hundred and sixty metres. He was well within it, but he was a better shot with a pistol than a rifle. He scrambled up to a vantage point and lay down. The Rover was hurtling down the track. They would've heard the gunfire.

Wilké lost sight of it as it slid around a corner.

He fought to bring his breathing under control once again. He pushed his body flat on to the ground, and propped himself up on his elbows. He sited the rifle at the point where he'd next see the Rover. It would be a side-on shot, at perhaps two hundred and fifty metres. After that he might get one more, but it would be at the rear of the vehicle, and at a greater distance. Then they would be around the last bend, over the stone bridge, onto the main road, and . . . free. Wilké's heart thumped against the confines of his chest.

Slowly in, slowly out.

The Rover came back into sight and Wilké squeezed the trigger. The rifle kicked into his shoulder, but the vehicle continued. He aimed slightly to the front of it: another crack — another kick — another miss.

Then it was gone.

Wilké didn't hold out much hope for his last chance. He waited. The Rover was at least three hundred and fifty metres away now, a minute target.

Slowly in, slowly out.

Crack — kick — missed again.

He thumbed the selector to safe, dropped the rifle, jumped up, and sprinted down the dirt track. There was no point in firing again. He had to make the village as soon as possible. Inform the police. He drew the Beretta from his belt, holding it out the way as he ran.

He pounded down the track, losing sight of the vehicle as it rounded the last bend before the bridge below. One mile. He couldn't do it in four minutes, but he thought he might make six. He was glad he'd shed some weight after Moon and Sommer had turned up at his house. He'd allowed himself to get fat and soft after Italy. He fought to get his panting into some kind of rhythm, fought to keep his legs and feet pumping like a piston.

He couldn't see the Rover yet. He might get one last glimpse as it turned onto the road and entered the village. His knees ached. He ran on.

He rounded another bend in the track. He saw the road and the village below clearly, but no Range Rover. It must be in the village already. Long gone. Another corner loomed ahead.

Wilké's shirt was soaked and the sweat poured off his eyebrows, stinging his eyes. One last corner, one more to go. Fifty metres from this bend, the bridge, then the road, and about a hundred more metres to the village. Nearly there.

He picked up the pace, driving his thighs up and down. He saw the bridge . . . closer . . . saw the banks of the Glaslyn River . . . heard a noise . . .

'Yer fecking eejit!'

Wilké slowed down, walked, cocked the Beretta. He was twenty metres from bridge. Three heads popped into view: Mullen and Connor dragging Padraig up the riverbank. Padraig's face was covered in blood and his legs sagged under him. Wilké saw the rear of the Range Rover protruding from the water behind them. Connor had taken the turn too quick, crashed. Mullen swore at him again. Connor had a pistol in his hand, Mullen an M4 slung over his shoulder.

Wilké stopped at the same time as Connor saw him. Wilké raised the Beretta as Connor's pistol came up.

Wilké fired — one round — two rounds. The cracks were soft compared to the M16.

Connor dropped Padraig. Mullen dropped Padraig.

Connor fell — bucking as both rounds struck him.

Wilké turned to Mullen. He had the M4 in his hands.

Wilké fired — once. Mullen knelt, brought the M4 up.

Wilké fired again. Mullen fired.

Wilké felt a dull thud in his abdomen — on the right hand side. Then his right leg buckled. He was staring up at the clear sky, lying on his leg. He moved his right arm to point the pistol at Mullen, but he'd dropped the weapon. He waved an empty hand at Mullen. He was confused. He saw Mullen standing over him. He saw the barrel of the M4 directly above his face. He heard gunfire — then everything went black.

Plas Gywnant, Tuesday 12th July, 0944 hours

'There it is again! Is it them, is it them?' asked Jessica from the backseat.

'I don't fucking know!' shouted Moon.

'I haven't heard that much gunfire since eighty-two — an' I weren't happy about then, neither — but I reckon those prats in Wrexham came through for us,' said Sommer as he drove.

'Look, up there! Tha' Land Rover's goin' dead fast.

'He's scarpering, that's what he' doing. Come on, John!' Moon picked up the mike, gave their location, and called for armed back-up.

'He's spooned, he's spooned!' cried Jessica.

'I wish you'd speak English,' said Sommer, as he powered the Astra up the road past Llyn Dinas.

'He lost it! The driver lost it on the

bend!' Jessica couldn't contain her excitement.

'Pukka.'

Moon put the mike back and drew his Glock. Jessica followed suite. 'Two of them have climbed out. What can you see, Jess? Macnamara?'

'We're too far. There's three of them. The other two are carryin' a third. I dunno who.'

Sommer had his foot flat, and Moon could see the men clambering up the riverbank.

'Wait, tha's Wilké. Wilké's just come round the corner!' Jessica could just make out Wilké on the other side of the track.

'Stop here!' Moon shouted to Sommer as he cocked the Glock. Jessica was way ahead of him. The Astra skidded to a halt. There was gunfire from across the river. Jessica saw three men drop. Sommer whipped up the handbrake. More gunfire. Moon and Jessica were both out while the car was still sliding. Sommer popped the boot, and debussed two seconds after them.

Moon and Jessica charged for the bridge.

Sommer took the Heckler & Koch submachine gun from the boot.

Moon surged ahead of Jessica. He saw Wilké on the ground and Mullen walking towards him. He sprinted.

Sommer flicked off the safety catch, and cocked a round into the chamber.

Mullen stood over Wilké. Moon — halfway across the bridge — stopped and raised his pistol. Jessica stopped beside him, knowing full well they were too far for an accurate shot. They both opened fire: two shots — three — four, five, six.

Sommer, still standing on the main road, eased the Heckler & Koch into his shoulder.

Mullen turned to Moon and Jessica. Moon fired another wild burst and missed. Mullen raised his rifle. Jessica took careful aim.

Sommer put a single round into Mullen's head.

Jessica ran over to Mullen. Moon followed. Brain and bone were protruding from Mullen's head. She kicked the M4 rifle out of reach. Wilké was lying on his back, unconscious.

'See what you can do for Wilké,' said Moon as he ran to the riverbank.

Once the shooting had started, Jessica had forgotten about the other two Irishmen. Tunnel vision, it could be fatal. She holstered her Glock, and knelt down next to Wilké. 'Wilké! Wilké, can you hear me!' She found the wound, hesitated when she realised she wasn't wearing gloves, and then covered it with both hands. She straightened her arms and used her bodyweight to increase the pressure. 'Wilké, Wilké!' She realised she didn't even know his real name.

Moon took the weapons from the brothers as Sommer appeared at his shoulder. 'Mullen and Connor are on their way out.'

'This one's in a right mess, an' all,' Sommer prodded Padraig with his foot.

'Nice one.'

'You're not wrong,' Sommer moved over to Jessica.

'Come on, Wilké, stay with me! Come on, my man, stay with me!'

He didn't look good. Sommer heard sirens and screeching tyres as the other

Special Branch personnel arrived.

The first police car slid to a halt in cloud of dust and gravel. Moon came over to Sommer, 'Is he gonna make it, John?'

'I dunno, guv, I dunno.'

Hit and Miss

Jessica Smith switched on her hands-free. 'DS Smith.'

'Jess — Harold — where are you?'

Not a best beginning to the conversation. 'M6 northbound, just passed Junction 14. I'm on my way back to Everton,' she added, in case Detective Chief Inspector Johnson had forgotten that he'd given her permission to do one a couple of hours ago.

'Good. I want you to divert to Snow Leopard's three-zero ASAP. Do you need directions?'

These codenames, where the heck did they get them from? 'Snow Leopard' lived in Buxton, gateway to the Derbyshire Dales. 'No, I'm on my way. Wha' is it, sir?'

'His security threat level's gone up to amber. New intel that he's the target for another kidnapping. No confirmation of timing or suspects.'

Seven months ago *al-Qaeda* had planned the kidnap of a Moslem British soldier, but the West Midlands Special Branch got there first and made eight arrests. 'Is this connected to the Birmingham cell?'

'We don't know. The target is different, obviously, but the plan exactly the same: kidnap him, and videotape his trial and execution.'

Counter Terrorism Command had been on top of the situation since the 7/7 wake-up call — until the car bombs in the Haymarket and Glasgow airport. But none of those had exploded and it'd been an unsuccessful year for *al-Qaeda* on both sides of the Atlantic. That could all be about to change, however, because a recent MI5 investigation had identified at least eight *al-Qaeda* spies in police forces across the UK. A plan to abduct and kill a former CTC agent was not in the least far-fetched. Not any more. 'Okay, wha' do I tell him?'

'Exactly what I've told you. You can mention Zulu Twenty-Two, but it's not definite. Derbyshire HQ and his local nick have been informed, and patrols will be routed to his three-zero on a regular basis — neighbourhood and armed response. You'll have to speak to him every day and visit once a week, starting tonight.'

Zulu Twenty-Two was the codename for the Abu Hafs al-Masri Brigade and the problem with that particular group was that no one knew whether it genuinely existed. Either it was *al-Qaeda's* most covert branch, or an invention, part of the wider campaign to instil fear into the public. 'I'll be there in abou' an hour,' said Jessica.

'Step on it. We've not been able to reach him by phone, and the locals have already knocked on his door without success. Find him, tell him, and let me know when you're done.'

'Wilco, sir.'

He hung up and she swore softly.

She'd been dead pleased when Johnson let her leave the office early. Now there was no way she'd get to her mom's before ten. No wonder they couldn't get hold of Jackson. He and his wife would be out and about, like normal people on a Friday night. She swore again. The worst of it was, she'd been his handler for less than a month. They'd neither met nor spoken. The last time she'd seen him was two years ago, when he'd been unconscious, lying in a pool of his own blood in the Welsh mountains. Jessica wasn't exactly sure what had happened in between, except that he'd done some sketchy job for the CIA that'd spooned. She didn't know the details, only that he'd managed to piss off three intelligence agencies, almost ended the career of his previous handler, and been promoted to the top of the *al-Qaeda* hit list.

What did Johnson expect her to say? *Hi, I'm DS Jessica Smith, your new handler. I've just stopped by to tell you that the AHMB plan to behead you on telly. We're not sure when, but don't worry, I'll be phoning you every day to check if you're still alive. I'll know you're not if you don't answer, or when I see you on BBC News 24. Enjoy your weekend*. She indicated to leave the motorway. We don't actually protect these people very well. On top of which we give them naff codenames. 'Snow Leopard', what was that all about?

Jessica tried Jackson's home number, and heard his wife's American accent on the answering machine. She identified herself and left a message for both of them to contact her ASAP. She tried his mobile, then his wife's; two more messages. She rang her mom next and told her not to wait up. At least she didn't have to identify herself a fourth time.

* * *

Lynley steered the Tigra convertible into Birch Tree Grove. 'Hey, what's the matter?'

Jackson scratched the scar on his cheek idly, and there was a pause before he answered. 'Nothing. I'm still surprised that Andy offered me the assistant manager's job after all the days I've had off. It couldn't have come at a better time. I don't think I'll be any good to mountain rescue for much longer; my hip hurts like hell and it's bound to get worse.'

'You don't know that, but you need to be more careful. And that means no more mountains, honey.'

'You know what really surprises me?' he turned to his wife, resting his hand on her long, firm thigh.

'Tell me,' she smiled.

'How much I'm looking forward to having a normal job, a regular life. I joined the security forces when I was nineteen; I've never known anything else until we moved here. Let's hope there aren't any more interruptions,' he stroked her leg through the flimsy silk skirt.

'There won't be. The Brits and the Agency both know to leave you alone now, and the South Africans have too many of their own problems. We'll be fine, you'll see.'

Jackson wasn't worried about interference from intelligence agencies, he was worried about retribution from terrorists — *al-Qaeda* especially. It was possible that they didn't know he'd been responsible for the death of four of their operatives, but he doubted it. He was also worried about the reports of spies in the police service. How safe were he and Lynley? On top of which the law of the land prevented him carrying a firearm to defend them. He had a Colt .45 in the house, but because of the need to keep it hidden, it would be of little practical use should an unexpected attack come. Perhaps he was over-reacting now that he was so close to the life he wanted.

Maybe Lynley was right.

Jackson watched her from the corner of his eye. Even after five years, he still found it difficult to believe she'd ever been his lover, let alone his wife. Physically, it was an unlikely match, and he couldn't remember where he'd found the courage to speak to her in the first place. Him, a chunky five-nine with a welt of scar tissue down his face; her, a leggy five-eleven who looked as if she'd stepped from the pages of *Vogue*. They'd both been in the Green Dragon Tavern in Boston, watching the New England Patriots. Jackson had always been an American football fan, and he'd probably been so caught up in the game that he'd just started talking to the stranger next to him without thinking. He'd not had time to be intimidated by her looks. Sometimes, an instinctive reaction was best. Thinking often meant hesitation — and hesitation could get you killed.

Lynley braked and turned into the tiny cul-de-sac at the side of their house. She avoided a white van parked under the ash tree, looped round in a neat semi-circle, and pulled up onto the short drive. The headlights illuminated their garage door, and Jackson noticed the hammer he'd propped against the fence on their way out. Lynley might be the most beautiful and intelligent woman he'd ever met, but she was also the most untidy. He often wondered how she could be the same person who ran a successful chartered architect's, and drafted extensive and meticulous plans with such ease. She'd left the hammer on top of one of the dustbins and he'd set it down next to the garage so he'd remember to put it away on their return. He looked at Lynley — she hadn't noticed — and climbed from the car. As soon as he closed the door, she initiated the roof and boot traction, which kicked in with a metallic whine.

Jackson picked up the hammer, realised his keys were in his left trouser pocket, and switched the tool to his right hand. He fished out the keys, shifting to one side so he could see the lock. He found the right key — inserted it — it wouldn't turn. Perhaps Lynley had forgotten to lock it when she'd left this morning. It wouldn't be the first time. Jackson gave the door a push, and took a step back as it swung upwards.

Two men stood in the garage, blinking in the beam of bright light.

Each carried a pistol.

Jackson drew back the hammer and hit the closest man straight in the forehead.

The sickly crunch of impact was drowned by the crack of a shot from the second.

The first screamed and crumpled.

Jackson heard a shout in Arabic from behind — he struck the second man, catching him in the temple. A grunt — two shots from behind — the roar of the Tigra's engine. Jackson hit the second man twice more as he fell, and his face and skull disappeared in a sheet of blood.

He crouched and spun on his heels.

Lynley reversed the car: a third man with a gun dived out the way, rolled, jumped up, and ran to the white van.

The tyres protested as Lynley slammed on the brakes.

Jackson strode towards the van, heard the engine revving. Lynley grated gears. He raised his palm, and shouted, 'Stay there! Get down and stay where you are!'

The van driver saw Jackson unharmed — panicked — floored his accelerator, left his accomplice behind.

Jackson hefted the hammer back.

The third man shouted — changed direction — sprinted in between the Tigra and the van.

Jackson hurled the hammer as hard as he could.

It smashed the glass of the driver's window: the van veered — bounced up onto the pavement — crashed into a lamppost.

* * *

Jessica saw the Town Inn and knew she was close. She found Birch Tree Grove and started looking for number thirty-nine. The houses on the left were in the teens, those on the right the seventies; how was anyone supposed to find anything? She'd have a major cob on by the time she eventually located the Jacksons. It was all the cul-de-sacs that cacked up the numbers. Jessica tried the third one and realised her mistake immediately. She rolled down her window for a better look at the houses and heard a car backfire somewhere further up the road. Actually, it was a bit loud for that.

Another bang.

Must be fireworks.

The sound of a car wheelspinning, the screech of brakes, shouts, the tinkle of breaking glass.

Jessica swung her Audi around, unclipped her seatbelt, and drew her Glock. She selected second gear and drove up Birch Tree Grove with the pistol cradled in her lap.

Footsteps — someone running — a figure burst into view a few metres ahead

— charged the car.

She braked — pointed the Glock over the steering wheel — shrieked at the top of her voice: 'Armed police, freeze!'

The man kept coming — raised his fist — cried: '*Sharmoota*!'

Too late, Jessica saw the gun.

* * *

Jackson was at the door in seconds. He wrenched it open, grabbed the driver, threw him down. He was on the man before he landed, punching his face — one, two, three, four, five times. He kept hitting until there was no more movement.

Jackson sprang up and opened the back of the van. Inside there was a steel ring bolted to the floor, manacles, handcuffs, two boxes, a rucksack, and a Samsonite case. He turned to the Tigra. Lynley was nowhere to be seen. Perfect. 'Can you hear me!'

'Yeah, I'm here,' she shouted from the car.

Jackson glanced at the three bodies

— one on the road and two in the garage — one twitching, the others still. He made a split-second decision. 'Go inside, pick up the black briefcase, a pair of walking shoes, and the .45. I'll meet you out front.'

She switched off the car, and dashed into their back garden.

Jackson saw neighbours peering from behind curtains.

He picked up the Samsonite case, dropped it in the Tigra, and raced to the garage. The first man was moaning, the second silent; neither were in any condition to fight. Jackson saw a Taser stun gun and a 9mm pistol, a compact Zigana. He retrieved the pistol, eased the hammer down, and slipped it into his jacket pocket. Then he ran back to the car and drove to the front of the house. Lynley arrived with the briefcase in one hand, and a carrier bag in the other.

She jumped in, 'Where are we going?'

'The FBI office in London, I've got a present for them.' He pulled off as she closed the door. 'I've still got friends there; they'll keep us safe.'

* * *

Jessica saw the muzzle flash.

She returned fire through the windscreen; the noise was deafening.

The suspect kept coming.

She fired twice more: double-tap.

His head jerked back — he dropped the gun — collapsed.

She whipped up the handbrake, debussed, and rushed to him. She saw he was bleeding, kicked his pistol into the gutter, and bent down to examine him.

Dead.

Her ears were still ringing and all she could hear was the thumping of her heart. She felt sick. She swallowed, took the Glock in both hands, and jogged up the road. Jessica saw the white van first: streetlight askew, vehicle smashed.

A blue Tigra hurtled towards her, two people inside.

She raised the Glock, 'Stop! Armed police, stop!' Somebody please stop.

The car skidded, darted off to the left, mounted the pavement, and bolted past.

Jessica turned, saw it fly round the

corner, and ran back to her Audi. She thought she heard more shots, but she couldn't be sure because of the ringing.

She reached the bend and saw the dead suspect, her car, and the Tigra stopped beyond.

A man who could have been Jackson dropped a handgun onto the road, climbed into the Tigra, and sped off for town.

Jessica leapt into the Audi, shut the door, put the Glock in the side panel, and gunned the engine. She slammed the car into reverse, stamped on the accelerator, and slid round into a cul-de-sac. The car swerved violently, but she corrected — braked — changed into first — and stamped on accelerator again. The Audi pulled right — Jessica counter-steered, narrowly avoiding a parked car. She swore, stopped the vehicle, and jumped out. Just as she feared: Jackson had shot out both tyres on the driver's side.

She never saw him again.

About the Author

Rafe McGregor was born in 1973 and educated at UNISA and the Open University. He worked in law enforcement in South Africa and England for eleven years before becoming a freelance writer. He and his wife, Linda, live in a village near York, in the north of England. Rafe is a member of several literary societies and his interests include military history, philosophy, martial arts, and the outdoors.

We do hope that you have enjoyed reading this large print book.

Did you know that all of our titles are available for purchase?

We publish a wide range of high quality large print books including:
Romances, Mysteries, Classics
General Fiction
Non Fiction and Westerns

Special interest titles available in large print are:
The Little Oxford Dictionary
Music Book, Song Book
Hymn Book, Service Book

Also available from us courtesy of Oxford University Press:
Young Readers' Dictionary
(large print edition)
Young Readers' Thesaurus
(large print edition)

For further information or a free brochure, please contact us at: